BLUE LIGHT

and

STARTING OVER

BLUE LIGHT:

AFTER THE END

STARTING OVER

John Fraser

AESOP Modern
Oxford

AESOP Modern
An imprint of AESOP Publications
Martin Noble Editorial / AESOP
28 Abberbury Road, Oxford OX4 4ES, UK
www.aesopbooks.com

ISBN: 978-0-9927588-5-1

CONTENTS

PREFACE

We all know what the end of the world is like – it's not dissimilar to our own end. In our heads, both these ends – the world, the person – are already present. *Blue Light* shows what it's like, the running down, the onset of *rigor mortis* – and the new life sprouting, notwithstanding. That is how it is, exactly so. The way it all happens.

Here, we're in Italy, where there's a high priest who's infallible; organised crime that's organised better than anything else; politicians who seem eternal, like the capital. Living in the capital, the Eternal City, you need Capital, and this is how it's generated and handed round.

Art too is eternal, so they say. Italy is full of it, some of it in fair condition. The process of producing it, or not quite finishing (and getting Capital for it too) – that's an even longer eternity.

The Eternal, the Immortal: as you'd expect, the gods and goddesses, demigods and nymphs, sylphs and mythic mortals, they're still around, and going strong. In every bar and cane brake, divinity is imminent.

At the start, the Professor's point is that 'isness', the present, the real, seems the tangible product of two unreal states – the past (wobbly memory, vacillating history),

vii

and 'blue land', the future. Blue land is hypothetically an 'end', our self-destruct – but of course, it's not 'real', it's as open to interpretation and construction as is the past. In this concoction, as the scene is Rome, the old gods and goddesses are present – immortal not as characters, but because the emotions they invoke and represent – love, jealousy, repugnance – are, for humans, immortal.

*

Living for ever may not be too bad – but do you really want it? When the world has ended, how attractive is rebirth, or resurrection? *Starting Over* may mean you have to piece a whole new world together – just using the ruins of the past. A drink, a smoke – that at least you need, but much is scarce or lacking, and what there is may not be good for you. And yet, it all comes sprouting up again! Is this hope? This unstoppable fecundity, an eternal recurrence we, this time, are conscious of, directing it, or so it seems – should we encourage it? Is this a false start? Perhaps the world that fell – or was pushed – wasn't worth reproducing. *Starting Over*'s cold 'I' moves among the highest authorities of the new dispensation, and is sceptical about it all.

An end requires the candle flame, at least, of something lingering on, or coming back. The flickering consciousness returns from its – maybe useless – operation and anaesthesia, carrying with it every memory, every place, relationship, song and dance. There's joy in this return?

BLUE LIGHT

AFTER THE END

De l'éternel azur la sereine ironie
Accable, belle indolemment come les fleurs,
Le poète impuissant qui maudit son génie
A travers un désert stérile de Douleurs.

L'azur, Stéphane Mallarmé

Je parlerai du revenant, de la flamme et des cendres.

Jacques Derrida,
De l'esprit. Heidegger et la question.

Rome

The Lecture

'I won't ask why there's something rather than nothing, since we're all hoping to find some lunch,' says poor old Professor Harmless – some German name – fishing for laughs. 'So I'll just ask, "Why is everything as it is and not something else?"'

'Silly old fool,' I think, 'everything is quite different,' as I'm eyeing, pulling on, that girl over there.

'You're mafia, aren't you?' she asks.

'Some silly people say I am, so what? There's a stigma. Some silly people say I'm not, they're still silly.'

'It's my dad,' she says. 'He's got some smelly cash,' and I say,

'It's mostly smelly. Banks have a scent they spray, otherwise you'd not go past, nor in – sniff the new notes, there's no drugs, no sweat, just clean and tidy.'

There is a pause, then I say, 'Of course I'm not mafia, just invest.'

Well, I wouldn't say if I was, or would I? Intervention, the investment stuff – it doesn't change a thing, like the prof says, just brings forth some more isness. Change, like he says, is an illusion, going on like birth or like decay, spring and whatever follows – even if nothing does – all's still firmly in the isness slot. It gives you something to hold on to – isness, the everything.

I say, 'There's commission.'

'Much?'

'For you, thirty per cent,' and she says,

'That's OK, it's just like taxes.' She thinks it's commission on the interest, not the capital: who cares, capital is soft as butter, spread it thick or thin, and in the end it's all chucked into Capital that keeps the world a-going round, deciding who is up and who is not or has been once.

'Where did your father get the cash?' I ask.

'Importing women and children. In rags. And beating them. And stealing what they earn.'

'OK!' I say, what I don't know won't hurt her, and I'll give her documents – that capital's like butter, and when it melts, it's gone, but – there's old Capital, it licks its lips, and down it's sunk!

'I'll give you documents,' I say. They're useful, keep your feet warm on the park bench. Or even – maybe you'll earn, we'll take a slice each year off what you give us, and there! It's all yours, – though it's all ours too. Don't ask too much.

How fortunate for her – not mafia, I just invest.

Apocalypse

I

So – no eternal return, no vengeful god, angels and flaming swords and justice. Just the eternal peace. The bodies, seen them a hundred times before – whole cities – bombarded and quite flat, like earthquakes pass, and there's a decency, for most are just gone under masonry. Leaving nothing, nothing written, not a diary, not a scroll, just – gone under, like foxes going down their hole.

A street directory, to show who lived in here, in there? a silence, absolute – but no! There's always author's footfalls, the witness, always the tourist, a chronicler, waving a two-by-four for safety, stumbling along, and all the guys and gals gone down, requesting nothing, not a word to leave, or grease the passing.

It's apocalypse, complete, it seems, with all gone down and all stashed somewhere out of sight, and all the shops still open, no problem for the food, and here are florists: you can pick yourself a suit, a pair of Chinese shoes.

There's no one here. They – we – were all warned, you'll bring the whole invention crashing down, the civilisation, armies, security, protection – all will go, and you'll go with it, and so you'll learn, you rueful shades that stand at desk and counter, smiling a little, nodding as I cart the stuff away – it's my necessity, you shades! you smile a little, nod, as off it goes – you couldn't take it with you, but we can – and do!

None but the invisible dead, in this flat city. Lucky me, to be alive, if that is what I am. Maybe accompanied, there's someone, presence with me, as I slide through, into this blue land, the end has come and gone, like me, I come and go, after the apocalypse, and every time there is some difference, although nothing's changed. No smell of death, no puppy dogs survived, miraculous, putting up a paw, or fangs more likely, no unseemly flapping dead in trees or in those doll's houses, razored open, bad taste on view – 'those pictures, well! my dear! – a view of gloom, if ever!' – drunks in glicée, watercolour tree – and is that sheep or rock?

But all gone far beyond the pity or the criticism – it's all just gone, it's like the other civilisations they say there were, just piles of rocks, no bodies, nothing, not a puppy dog, no Roman cinemas that show an early movie, porno, probably, extreme sport, gladiators, or slaves that do some dirty things – you have to face them the next day, they bring you tea in bed, and they'll be there tomorrow and for ever, all your life, lives of their descendants, some immured for sacrilege, some stuck with spears in sandy bowers where the itch of conquest drives – but mostly living out short lives, bit of hardcore in the servants' attic. This is their hope, your hope, this, the ideal. And now they're gone, you're gone, it's all quite silent.

Those bombs, invented, waiting to be used – for now 'unthinkable' but stocked up somewhere, manicured by men and women who are quite real and thinkable – those bombs they say would leave the buildings, kill the people. That's what it's like, like it happened here, in this blue land.

What good are buildings without people? Waiting for some hussars, some cossacks, to come and stable horses in them. Would they have killed the animals too, those bombs? – I think the living things would all be vaporised, or else there'd be those corpses – not the clean deal that they promised us. And plants – living things, but maybe bombproof? – the people, they've all gone, so who's to tell if it all worked? Maybe they've all gone to hide.

That's the effect here – as if the people other people hate had all been executed, not even camps and ditches, but everyone who hates someone and is in turn a hated person – no hope, no chance!

I hear you scheming: 'That religion or that sect, that struggles against its hostile thoughts, or maybe's just indifferent, or doesn't even know the signs of who they must exterminate, maybe there's too many kinds of guy even to discriminate – those colours, creeds, ethnicities, abundance – Yes,' you say, 'Get rid of all of those, and more, the ones whose chatter wakes me up, who stand in front so I must wait or not get served, who get my misdirected mail, who eat the food I might have liked, who are unjust or maybe finicky, their hearts are on their sleeve, or maybe want my charity' – well, they're all gone. And so are you.

It can't be bombs. Here, almost all have left, the traffic, and the soldiers, old and young they've just decamped, or gone to dust.

There are the shades. In shops they don't exactly help, don't ask for cash, but there they are, behind the counter, weary, flyblown, worldly-wise and stuck in grooves, as if behind those counters they'd become an architecture, attached so hard and fast, they don't have sentiments, or pleasures, they're like shavings, they live on, hearth spirits of the store.

Not every shop. I find my card works in the banks, the cashpoints, though I don't remember any credit anywhere, or balance, inside there is no one. No bus, no plane. No cars, no bicycles. No way to leave. No other people. Just us two. If two we are, in this blue light it's hard to see. Not every shop – just for my necessities, my food – it's fresh or freshly packed, preserved. No books, no papers, naturally. No time, no change, just things becoming different each time, each time I – we – visit.

No butchers, so there's nothing left to butcher – as for clothes, I can get by a year or two with what I've got. It's all quite basic, but I'm not so squalid I think the whole show's put on just for me, a silent quiz of all these shades, they take me down a can of that, a pack of this – just so's I can get by.

It's quiet, like I have never heard it, with no machines, no wind, no birds, no leaves asleep or turning on the branch. I'm not alone, there's you, of course, beside me, eating too. It's not unpleasant, but I've never been so lonely, with no wish to change it.

Apocalypse has come. And gone.

There being only food to keep us occupied, we eat and eat – we're quite the connoisseur, the gourmand and the gourmet too, we stuff ourselves, and air is spurtling out to make some room, a little organ-pipe of quick among the absent. Our mouths are full to sticking, with our eyes we ask, 'Where are they all, and was it fast or painful, who's responsible? Can't be willed, not suicide, or not on purpose, maybe things ran out, water, air, the will? or was it just the usual, collision of forces, or of interests, that didn't know the way to stop until it was too late, too many homicides topped off with suicides, some

ordinance removing every corpse?' – a word that seems
obscene, unseemly: corpse.

There's nothing here, just nothing, and the shades in
stores – no bars and no cafes – to help us eat, they used to
say: to keep our body and our soul together – maybe the
souls flew off? – and then I think, yes, there are bars, and
restaurants, the structures all in place, and when I say
'there's nothing' I just mean – the people. They are not.
Not missed and not recorded, mourned or celebrated –
and who cares? Another generation passing, passed into
nothing, into the chain of being, or of evolution, or just
eating – so, who's to mourn? and what's the point? the
dead are in no hurry to do anything, nor do they tip their
hats, make dates. They're gone, just like the people here.

*

I go into this hall, it has a dome – a terminal, they're
called, bus or train station maybe, though no one's coming
in or going anywhere.

I blow my food out on the floor, – marble, colour of
mortadella, pink and white and not quite wholesome.

*

I scream and scream, a monkey's scream. The sound goes up, umbrellas out along the roof ribs, cascades down and into every little kiosk, through the holes in manholes, up the spouts where drinks come out of the machines, it fades back in my ears, falls, dies, and leaves no trace. It's swallowed up by something, no one's there to know that it has ever been.

What a sound! No trumpet could do better.

No dead to wake, the angels, if they'd ever been, they won't return, they folded up the breathing things, off with them

and

it's over. Worst has passed and left this perfect, this eternal, peace.

*

We're back. This girl and I. We chat, I say,

'No! Not him? You didn't fuck with him!' Amusement, probably simulated. I go on, 'He wears pants of – well, it could be herringbone. From those boutiques, near "barbers' salons"! And those thick shoes, the welts stick out. Roumanian shepherds wear them.'

'Well, of course he takes them off,' she says, her look is far away, or maybe just remembering – our walk, together, the blue land. 'Anyway, it's not his clothes.

Maybe his father dressed like that.' I agree, fuck his clothes, and him too.

*

The village, where I live. The village, full of time and power.

They say Napoleon lived here, these tiny rooms, all now restored, in 1930s kitchen style. Across a little lake, another village opposite and similar, as if it's pasted on a view.

Half the houses are in ruins, all set on rock without foundations, Roman style – without expectations, just stones and rubble piled up, reusable if all falls down.

Here, Napoleon watched his mistress in the villa over there – then, world spinning on, the Duce watching his. A car-ride from the city, here for a midnight gallop, roads just tracks, darkness of scuttering animals.

The house is let, here's a couple, cellist and violist, they're playing. I go in and say, 'That could be Shostakovich.'

'Lots of this stuff, you don't know who it's by, people afraid let slip their pieces under pseudonyms,' and the girl, the violist, says, 'It's pitched too high. The fear, maybe. As if it's on a slope.'

The guy has hold of my arm, he shows me furniture and says, 'That there's a secretaire. In the well you could hide someone, a secretary, maybe,' he gestures, paints the picture of two naughty eyes, some pants, sweaty, dropped – 'Just make an offer!'

On tippytoes, I sidle off. Those musicians, fixed in the age of donkey cart – those fiddles! – venerable instruments! – I think of them; the village; rent to pay – they seemed a couple twinned in incest, fiddling, a duo terrified, and I think:

'O no, not love story,' maybe theirs is, but that stuff belongs in those back centuries, and all gone now – raw lives that were: this pair, musicians, don't belong. The peasants, mothers, sisters, lying like bolsters in iron beds, – or passion in the fields, some minutes in the lifetime. A brother, head of clan maybe, and knifed, the whole gang surging forward in revenge, ants running marathons, and every leg is running, fast as it can – all peasant civilisation, all the *ritornelli*, taken from the top again.

Those tenants, they've not a mark to leave on all that time. Their fear, teetering at the top, the slope. The snotty smell of cannabis. Selling the accessories, the furniture. Fiddling in old Boney's house.

Is there some journey here, a Gilgamesh, a start and finish, even somewhere transiting? Shades. We go in search of them, they seem to cheer us up. Music a thumbprint in the clay.

*

I ask the girl – after the lecture, and her father's cash:

'Now, the apocalypse? The land? We were there, together, then? You? Yes, of course you were. I didn't see you.' And she says,

'Those shades, those people who just seemed appendages, who can they have been?'

I haven't got a clue. I say,

'Think of those Etruscans – it's all genes, they linger on. Once they were singers, dancers, for the Romans. I guess you go to Aztec or to Mayan lands, you'll find them hanging on, not heroes, not sacrificed or farmers, but they're there, belong to something older, all gone under, irretrievable, past that's really passed ...'

She ponders this. 'I think they were just the ordinary – people you don't look at, for you they never leave their context, guys who sit for ever stamping tickets, two-dimensional, like marquetry, the master, magister, integral to their hole. And now, they sit before a screen, and even more attenuated, don't have a dimension now at all,' and she sinks deeper in her imagining. I try to pull her out as she sinks down and down. She's quite sucked down, but in my eyes there's coils of herringbone, sloughed off, the shoes apart, in excitement maybe or just careless, bound to traditions in the clothing – her bright eyes underneath that uncouth flesh, or maybe riding high. That guy. I think, goddam, the wanting and the hating come together like a pair of gloves, the best instant's projected over and over – another scene, double exposure, another cut.

You're there and having a good time – but so is someone else, the sketch beneath the picture, hidden and always present, then …

'Snap out!' she says, 'Get busy with the cash!'

'I'm off to my piano lesson.'

'Off you run, then. How strange.'

'I don't need to run, I walk. I give them.' Then,

'I'm composing,' I say, unnecessarily. 'Prepared piano.'

She laughs, 'And if you catch it unawares?'

I say, 'It's a special thing. You wouldn't understand – though you could look it up.' She asks,

'How good are you? How do you have time?'

'When I play, one thing leads to another – the chords, I'm doing Scarlatti and it turns to Ligeti. The audience don't follow – it's a kind of jazz, a soup. And then I find it's something someone's done before and got the critics in to hear. I'm a monkey at the typewriter – or that guy who wrote *Don Quixote* again, like the original, identical, made a story of it, what a bore! And as for time – when I've shot some guys and done insurance fraud and stolen some identities – there's still time left for music skills.'

I'm obsessed by her bed habits, and I say, 'You just screw, while we're at work?'

She says, 'It doesn't really mean too much, you can't put out a sign. Nothing's produced, no skill, it's really vanity,' and I put in, 'And having dinners paid.'

'Sometimes I pay – my father's got a lot of cash. But I don't enjoy that, it's not the taste I want.' Loftily, I say, 'You're one of those women the bourgeoisie have in common, then?'

'I suppose so, though I've never really understood it. Some women are available as objects of desire and general attachment.'

*

'I've never seen you naked,' I say.

'Fancy's free,' she says.

So's jealousy, with all its squirming actors.

She says, 'Jealousy's not worth it,' and 'What does your family do? Mine gets rich.'

I tell her, 'We were well off. A cold tap in the kitchen, latrine on the terrace. Straight-up chairs against the walls, a table lugged in for the notary, or a coffin when there was a wake. Murders. Suicides – who "fell downstairs" – and just the ordinary dead. Not a scrap of nakedness.'

'You're funny,' she says. 'But not enough.'

*

Of course, I'd no intention of handing her cash to someone else. That someone would be criminal, just like her father – so I do the collectivity a favour.

Sex – you become one flesh, like in theology. Then you get tired – that other body's just your own. You inhabit it. It's dull, it's everyday.

Jealousy, though! The other really is the Other, that writhes in turn with others – like the giant with writhing snakes. Penetrated at will by different guys, or gals, the loved one stays apart, no fusion for you there, but how you suffer! That body's violated each day, as often as you think of it, that itch you scratch and make it raw, no remedy. Until you turn to think of other things. The loved one: is that what they are? Or just desire, insatiable.

I'll have her cash. Desire without a respite while she frolics, stays forever other, out of reach, beyond a satisfaction. Cash is faith.

I'm the lucky one!

*

John Fraser

'Talking of families,' I tell her, 'there was a terrible
battle, between the Bashirs and the Jabils. The Bashirs
fought desperately to defend their fields, the Jabils to
take them. They say there were women who fought for
the Bashirs, and when it ended, each side had lost a
thousand warriors, and the proportion of survivors was
the same as the size of the armies at the start – 470
Bashirs and 390 Jabils. The Bashirs collected their dead,
but the Jabils left theirs, they went away, and no one
buried them, it was a dreadful sight, they say the
battlefield was like a living breathing blanket, black and
busy. Crows. They took off all the faces so they looked
the same, and no one of the Jabils came to gather up the
arms, collect the mail ... You're not laughing?'

'Oh absolutely not.'

'.... recover the armour.'

'And which are you, a Bashir or a Jabil?'

'You'll have to guess,' I say, offhanded and offended.
She thinks I tell her lies.

*

'I've the sadness on me,' she says, 'Like the curtain
beginning to fall.'

Her sadness. My money.

I say, 'If your father wants anything, I'll buy it for him. That's what banks do.'

'It's his money.'

'I don't see sweat on the notes. He gave it to me. I'll pass it round.'

She sniffs. 'Don't lose it.'

'If I lose it,' I say, laughing, 'Then it's his, it was.'

'I'm sad,' she says again.

To cheer her up, I say, 'Think of creation as a joke, all written out, and no one laughs, it's written quite perverse: the bible.'

'We don't read it,' she says.

I go on, 'Starts with this monster who can give you boils, put frogs down your caftan, then it ends with love and torture, some big bang hallucination. What way is that to live?' I pound along, she follows feebly, and I say, 'Those peasants fishing for the moon – they saw it in their well, and paid for it – and then there came the Wise Men with their pole and tried to hook the moon down from the sky – and then those guys, those two guys, on salary, we had them blasted up, they brought back – just rocks and dust.' I'm almost crying with delight, yes, this is joy – 'And we should think we've found the door, escape hatch and ejection, exit – hold on tight, we'll all be blasted off, out of this joke, into another where there doesn't grow a flower, no rats play there ...'

She says, 'I'm still sad. I'm not laughing. It's sadness written into poetry,' and she pleads, 'Not those creeds, those tall tales, please – it makes me fade away.'

*

Well, how shall I spend the money that guy's given me?

*

'It's not love it's all about,' she says. 'Why should it be? It's narrative drive, that's what it's all about – great epics – they're all about finishing the game, having a good end.'

'I don't want to disagree,' I say. 'But here's this book I read, it asks, is the past real, or is the future? The present, nothing you can grasp and keep – maybe it's best to think it's all unreal, like sleep. Your "real", it's clear, it isn't mine. It's different. In a word, it's sad.'

'You shouldn't hold it so against me.'

'Those epic guys and gals, the Sufi queens, messiahs, warriors – great lovers, but they're mostly cutting heads off whatisthis and whatwasthat, and suffering a lot, but never falling into sadness with it all, and not reflecting much on what the story line's about. "And what has that to do with time?" you ask' – but she's not with me, and I say, 'It's time that's passed, time wasted. Not for remembrance, but confection, like a cake, or omelette. Think of your life as sliding into custard – and hey! – here come some fresh ingredients – and dammit – there they go! You have to spend it as it comes.'

I'm thinking how to spend the cash, but still have more and more to come, like future – not try with that Wise Men's hook to snag it on some present or some past – that way, you're fooled. And end in sadness.

*

'I could have been called Ramona,' she says, 'my father was playing that when I was born, but instead they called me Venus. Childbirth was a joy. And I don't read the bible.'

*

We are in Istanbul. It's long ago, once more the sheep are grazing in the grounds of mosques – here is the Blue Mosque, there a flock, shoulders marked in orange, property of no one, here behind the rusting railings, safe for a while – from wolves, and dogs – a truce, those two bands of brigands on hind legs, staring at dinner milling round. There's menace here, I shuffle her away.

There's the hotel, I stayed there for a month, the waiter behind his pillar, popping out to say, 'Your special food.'

I didn't want it. 'I want Turkish food,' and he would say,

'Chicken, very good and very Turk – not Russian chicken,' and he mimed a knife across his scraggy neck. 'Turk chickens killed this way,' and we go in, look for a sign – there's scuffing near the pillar, but the waiter and the chicken's gone, and leaving nothing, whether he was East or West, if chicken met a halal end, it all seems trivial, maybe he's a boy again, and courting, watching the wrestlers in the Sweet Waters oiling up, belly dancers with their veils a-tinselling. The breeze.

He's on the balcony, an Armenian girl is watching him, a danger sweet as cakes. He's full with fantasy, delight – and doesn't try to cross the time, the distance, gives it up, the sweetness.

'Can you blame him?' asks Venus.

'Of course,' I say. 'What story's this? Besides, he was a timid guy, all crow, no cock,' and laugh – 'All blown away.'

We walk along the walls, we take the city, just like Turks.

*

It's not that Venus is unfaithful – while she's with me, she's being unfaithful to someone else. It's that she's inconstant.

Well, what do I expect?

All in the name, and her father – 'How's my little Venus?' getting off on his own invention, though his money's good.

Now, we're in that park, where I saw the guy with the violin, and they pressed notes into his hand, jostled, and then all the men around stood back, and he fiddled and sang some lampoon on someone, and we all marvelled and clapped – and of course he held his fiddle upright on his knee, you can't sing if you hold it Western style, under your chin. And when I told my friends, they said, 'There is no fiddler in the park' – well, what do you say, friendship is like that, and now there's no one there at all, you wouldn't trust your little Venus to run up and down these gravel walks, the trees bursting with pollen, musk. Here's a military jacket, 'Hero of Labour', a medal, maybe he's fought a war in it, then sweated more – they used to stand up for him and applaud in restaurants, made you forget the food and think of something else, and now it's cast off here.

What can you do with it, a castoff jacket? An overcoat, a nose – they're famous here for castoff things. Wouldn't want to start all that again.

*

'I like your stories,' Venus says, 'They don't depend on time – just don't get ideas,' and we are in the blue land now ...

She says, 'It may not happen, and not soon.'

'A little of it happens all the time.'

She looks at me, 'You're a funny oik.'

'All those tombstones, equal, standard issue, makes them – all those guys – seem just the same, as if there's something odd about each one that should be covered up – each one was different, did something that was different, his real – the tombs are overwhelming, all the same—'

'It's because they were comrades,' she interrupts. 'Willy-nilly.'

'And yet,' I go on, 'the cute ones, funny ones – those are the ones that make you pause, not these great military plains, these fields of wheat, stone plants.'

'Wheat that was threshed,' she adds, 'and now in stone, now, just the picture, no more harvested.'

'No market for stone bread,' I say. 'And with apocalypse – just empty space.'

'The organisation gives you purpose,' Venus says, 'you must know ...'

To me, the organisation's just some creep, bearing an envelope that buys me, vote or uniform, and when it's done with me, it drops me off.

'I didn't vote,' Venus says, 'I was doing something else. Besides, if there's no woman, I think – screw them all.'

*

It's an old zoo. I say, 'I won't go in. The horrors – now the people's gone, we don't need feel and suffer with them, I thought the animals had left as well, but then – those sheep, the dogs and wolves all waiting round, no safely grazing here.'

'Let's go in,' says Venus, she's more curious, and so we see – I guess the pigs and monkeys have a scheme, there's big beasts walking round but in the canopy the little bright and sensitive things are all a-chatter, some are screwing, others toss a cone, a nut, down on the lions and camels,

'They've worked it out,' I think, 'not to eat each other all at once,' they didn't need the keepers to teach them that.

'They've got it all worked out,' Venus says, and she is satisfied, but I'm less so, there is an air of 'nothing do and nowhere go', the best there is for them.

*

The mine! They used to make the nickel sleeves for
shells and such, an army of the guys down there, a city
with its notables and guys that drifted in and out, the
Indians – the unions think the Indians are useless, on
Monday you can see them, sit in rows, the drunken Indians
now sober in the courtroom – haha, just part of the culture,
not to be proud of, just let it roll right over you, not worth
analysis – besides, you Indians, you pass right over that
whole continent, like a wind that bends the corn in
waves, or else you live in tents and shacks and never
move, it just rolls on and over you, the time.

Time and space, they're empty – you must fill them
up with something.

The galleries, the chimneys up to nowhere in the rock,
it's huge, this emptiness – you think, in buildings what is
empty's part of structure, has a sense, but here, down
here, it's empty into emptiness, no punishment now, no
Monday justice, no people, useful and not, no union,
some guy wants to fight a class war – but it's all just
hollowing out, a burrow, tunnel for no animal, no home,
no rest when you have finished. Some hero, some class
war, to give a sense, and not just caste and hierarchy, bits
of cash to spend when you go up (it's dark, but you can
spend) – and nothing rolls for you, just 'fuck the Indians'

and blast away and lay the charge and hope it blows, it's hot down here, it's hot as where you wouldn't want to go.

So finely made, this rock, that sometimes splinters, flakes like salmon, and the colours: fleshed out like tuna, bronze of cuirass and greave, and then a blank, a blank face, not a seam or wrinkle, find some way round, beneath, the great dictator rock – then little goblin faces, blast it all away, another picture shows, all laid down in the rock.

Venus points into the blue, and says, perhaps in mockery, 'There's Indians down there', but there is no one, just the scribble on the walls – for dynamite, for women waiting up above – or maybe there are drawings, stick men, stick animals, before all those modern guys, machines. Maybe the early men, they came down here and prayed and painted.

'No, it's all modern,' I say. 'The faces in the rocks, the galleries, the blasting. Fed the city up above,' and Venus says,

'Don't be so wide-eyed! That's how it is, it was, you know it is.'

*

We've left the blue land.

Venus prompts me, 'People, just as memories – you must have some?'

'Just one guy – a Polish flier, at the opera. He must have been a hundred, brain had gone to broth, thought we were attacking him, there in the dark, must have thought he was up there, the sky, and had to drop his bombs on Ruslan and Ludmilla, couldn't keep him quiet, the old, the broken fool. He said, "O I fought – your president, your queen, be grateful, saved you all."'

'Whoever brought him there?' she says. 'And you must know some lighter guys, without the fear, some fighters, battles in the streets, the cops all fired with dope, young heroes with the big idea – the buses overturned, the gas, the gas.'

'All that,' I say, 'and markets too, those sacks of beans and roots, the Turcomans, the Tajiks, maybe buy a donkey or a knife for melons,' but she's lost, interest has gone, and time and place – it's all gone down, all that was never mine nor yours, passing became the past, and now the present skims like past; the future – we're not sure, but probably won't come, or if it does – ephemeral.

And now the people's gone, not fiction and not memory, but something radical.

It's all over, finished, it's the end.

*

'When I was a soldier,' I say, 'they gave me a slave, a pretty little girl. She was helpful, and we flourished,' and I wait for her riposte.

'Then what happened?' she asks.

'It's always "then" and "after". They say life's a rolling stream, but really it is lots of them.'

'It's time, time, you idiot! Not life,' she laughs. 'Why be a soldier anyway?'

'A dream of fun and duty – little of either, as it happens. The impact's through the eyes, and stops there, just freeze frames. Like walking through a city in an earthquake, everything has fallen down, things are hanging wrong way up – bad pictures on the walls, the nail still holds, but horizontals don't, the bed is hanging by a leg, and guys are pulling at you – crying out for help, info, hard luck tales. It's all disaster mode, the director's having fits somewhere, and who's in charge can't read or write, he has to get some other guys that translate what he thinks, all's out of synch, the music's lousy – if it's hot they sew you in a tortoise shell, and if it's cold you're in your skin ...'

It isn't what she wants to hear. 'That was a bad idea,' she says, and I think of where my plan is leading, nice to have a theme in life, like growing old or getting wise, even endure some treachery – but what I want is something quite precise – seducing Venus, quenching desire and what we speculate is love – both together. The ultimate in veneration, storming heaven. Being master.

But she must want to be seduced. Then, there's the 'after'.

'Duty'? 'Seduction'? Going for a soldier – what romance is this – you go, and what comes back? Maybe you, or maybe nothing. Romance, romance.

I think, well, money for certain has its future.

Venus says, 'You'll have to meet my father', so I go.

*

Sharp, he is, sharp as a stoat's nose. Tall flowers in his garden, machines for tending them. 'My little girl,' he says, and laughs. 'Her future. Just you wash this stuff,' and he points to some money, a lot, 'Hear its confession, then forget it. Buy her a convent in the mountains, with a fair return ...'

I join the joke: 'Why bother – just go on and spend it, everyone will love you so.'

'I told you, it's for her,' he says. 'They love me more if I don't spend, and once it's gone, she has no claim, no claim at all,' and she seems pleased, delighted. That is love and joy.

'It's all a preparation,' I tell him, and he's not impressed.

'They all say that,' he says, 'the suitors, and I tell them, "find another lie", my goddess, angel, sleeps with who she wants – and their ambition isn't worth a deuce,' and he gestures raking in a pile of chips. 'Maybe one day I'll be called – commander of the Western army. Even the Centre, or the East – a bit of soldiering will give you just the edge when you are called to loose the hounds of war. And once they're off, it's hard to call them back. It helps to have authority.'

Venus whispers, 'He's got all the cash you need – he's already got an army. Just a little one,' and her father goes on:

'Experience you need – but not of marching out in front, not like the bugler (lucky guy!), who gets to go in front and sound the charge. In your office, make the call, ring, ring, the hounds are off! It's like you see some guy, he's got a gun, so you must take it – in the system now, any two can beat the third – and so it's all political.' He smirks. 'You know, I've sat round tables, prayed to Fortune – you're always on your own, for that's the game. You pray to Fortune – that is in our nature, but you have to force her if you want to win – and someone always wins – and maybe Fortune has a pimp somewhere who tells her how the luck should fall, for force and flattery, all turns out the same. You're on your own, and someone always wins.'

As I leave, I see an old Corvette, buried in his gravel to the wheel arches. Tied to a handle, an old Bafra packet, Turkish cigarettes, used as a token, it says, 'I passed, I thought of you' to guys in jail, or maybe 'When you're out, you'd better watch for me, I don't forget.'

Her father says, 'Venus never means she has to be beautiful – it's not about beauty – she's Venus because she's my little goddess,' he doesn't mention, maybe doesn't see, the Bafra packet, though that's all I seem to see.

Venus says, 'My father? Man of mysteries? He never tells anyone anything.'

I say, 'It's difficult, fitting the pieces together,' and think, 'when there aren't any.'

She asks, amused, 'Whose army were you in?'

'They're much the same. Not introspective.'

Where did Turks come from, I wonder, how do they impinge?

*

I discover it, the big idea. Rather, container for lots of big ideas, and some of them are mine.

'It'll be – like a monastery.'

Venus says, 'You can forget that – poverty and early rising.'

'A retreat.'

'No.'

I explain, 'A hotel.'

'Too much drudgery – for you, too.'

'It's a place where the rich and powerful will come, and be austere, and give me money and their confidence, I'll be the guardian of their faith. There, in the mountains, by the lake, where the sea waves like ripe wheat, the pines, the oleanders, the sea eagles gyre over the red cliffs, and those mule carts heave the eager pilgrims up the slope and through the fields of flowers there – I'll direct it all...'

'It's sounding better,' she says.

'They think it was a solitude, but really, it's a place for them to keep an eye on rivals – and I shall hold the bets, unseal the cards, and deal them hands ...'

'Where will you get your slaves?'

'No slaves, a-sneering at their masters and calculating for freedom when the boss is dead. Those guys, the guests, they make a mess, they clear it up. As pilgrims, hermit crabs, they find a hole, and leave it clean. I shall inspect the scene, and make them pay.'

'And the money for all this?' she asks, and I don't say, 'It's there already,' but I talk of banks and stuff and

instruments, of credit and discredit, balance and crash
and cash, exchange and breaking banks, black cats and
the tarot – I spill out the medicines, the twisty tools you
need, the prayers, the runes, that serve to make you more
and more: money. But I'm the lucky one, I've got it all
already!

'What'll they do?' she asks.

'Philosophy. Self-justification. Courses on what they
are, and where they'll go, what to believe in. Spin the
long straw from finest gurus' nests – and make it gold!'

*

To celebrate, we'll go – to the blue land.

'I need some shoes,' she says, goes into a store, and
comes out with a sackful.

'They're all left ones,' I say, 'I'm doing fine with
these bits of leather,' but she sifts, we bicker, and she
says:

'I found a knife too – now, all we need's a place to
plug it in. And a pig,' but they will all have gone away in
herds, if they've any sense; besides …

I say, 'I can't work these machines.' All round there's
some that's huge, and others mute like brooches, not as
precious, but their story's gone – it makes me think.

'The first man was Iraqi,' I say, 'not a Turk.'

'The Turks will find it hard to take – and what's it to do with us?'

'We seem to be the last of something,' I say, and she's furious,

'Just get away! Don't get ideas, your trick is soldiering, not procreation,' and we sit on rocks, and wait for no birds, flying from left to right if possible, or just in gyres, and maybe they could lay some eggs. But all is sterile, perhaps beneath the sand and clay there's life that starts to ruminate, but who can wait?

I say, 'Of course, there's no one left to serve. Why should they linger round – for just two customers, who don't pay? They may be thin, but stupid, no – they've slipped away like things on film, or messages.'

'I like it silent,' she says. 'Not like this – it's got too meagre, pictures there are, and architecture, – but no sound, no movement, no people moving up and down, no panic, suffering – just contemplation.'

I say, agreeing, 'No search, so no beginning. What can we do here? Lots of food in packs, and stealing – though if there are no owners, can you steal?'

'And if you say we'll start some kids – forget it, that's not part of anything at all. We might find some ...'

I think, and do not say, that all the heroes start from total nothing – alone, a hillside, mountain cave, a shipwreck – but then adventure starts – a wise man, crone, a lion that talks, but here it's all closed down. Or else the hero's driven out, falsely accused, maybe some plot at court – but we've no court, no plot.

'There's still the arts of space,' I say, 'but there's no music, film – we fooled ourselves those weren't just space. Not real, not life, not movement – the guys responsible gone elsewhere, even dead, the final cut or chord – and then, what then? It's simulacrum, it's not life – a strip of tape, a page, and even when we set it up, the music's air, blown out or sawed, just waftings. Film – actors on wafers, screwing – a millimetre thick, in two dimensions – books too, what are they without eyes, the music without ears?' I sit, and know I'm saying what we know: 'a solitude'.

'Sadness,' she says, 'Quite irreversible.'

She goes on, 'I didn't know you were interested in all that, symphonies and such.'

'Of course not,' I say, 'nothing to do with that at all. I'm quite modern, in the music sense. That's what I've been telling you – memory turns to dementia, the past is like the future – neither exists, it's all fantasy, selection, telling tales. What you call real people, they just get in the way, and when they've gone – the only tiny movement's in the stuff they've left. The arts of space! Contrived and empty, I hate spectating ...' and Venus makes a pause, she's like a statue clothed in gold, her money – and she's complete, should understand.

'You're horrible,' she says, 'a boaster – you greedy horror! I'm quite real in all my lives, and so's my father, and his cash. You'll see – I am revered through all my twists and japes, and you – you're insubstantial, nothing but your tales. You gawp!'

'We have survived,' I say. Here we go, into the blue land, we're unique, the ones who made it, when the old world tumbled down, and no regrets.

I think back, I say, 'At its best, everything was, well, a mess.'

She says, 'They wiped themselves out. And I doubt we'll last for long. How do you begin again – from this?' she waves her arms, there's houses round, not beautiful, obscured, and shops. It's winding down, it's like the ink you need for copies running out, the too-much light that fogs the film, the secret ink that fades, stays mute, farewell that's grudging, scarcely meant, the stage left bare.

Must mean something, I suppose.

*

'I'm in my sad bubble again,' she says. 'It's all sad, the moving on, all that.'

'I'll snap you out of that,' I say, and lay on a quiet but pointed scene of jealousy. She's furious, and I wonder who is it says we shouldn't feel it, jealousy, since we do.

'You creeping thing,' she says, 'what is it that you think you want?'

'I want what drives the whole machine, war chariot, scimitars on the wheels.'

She's cured of sadness, happy, angry as a rattler, and she says, 'What's this with Turks? Because they're jealous too?'

'They were all over, biggest movie, lingers on in memory,' and I expound: conquest and occupation, long retreat, unspooling, bits of film cling to your hair, your clothes, it's static juice, you pull it off and there it springs, the more you fight, the more it clings ...

She says, 'If your retreat, the super hall, makes you a philosopher, a prince if not a king – you've started badly.'

'You have to learn it,' I say, 'we all do, we're all born without opinions of a fact that's worth a spit, and so we learn to live, well, philosophically.'

'Idiot – you just want power and cash.'

'A begging bowl and lots of fans. Or long life up a tree, or running deep inside, and finding voids that smell of musk.'

'The Turks,' she says. 'The more you have resisted them, the more you're like them, your bad side, and theirs.'

I think a while and say, 'Let's build the Venusberg first, then we can talk,' she doesn't find it fun or funny, but we seek out our mountain by the sea, the alp, the spar of sand, clear off the plastic binbags and the needles – there it will rise!

A bulb, a crocus bulb, that's blue and gold, on top shall there be minarets or pinnacles, some gargoyles, tasteful, rose windows in every room? – and does she know, her money's doing this, the price she pays? Philosophy, an hour of sex, or maybe two, and then unspooling, ready for the editing.

*

It's all built.

It's a dome of blown pearl glass, a mosque, basilica, that's lost its body, its thorax – it's all head and brain, and pinnacles jut out, like shoots on a potato, like baby horns. Horns of fortune and misfortune, gestures to ward off the minor gods misplaced – we cut down cane brakes where the rustic rituals were held, we'll never be forgiven, but don't care – hell is boredom, not torture, and we shall not be bored.

I tell Venus, 'Lots of American philosophers. They think I'm the front porter, they keep asking me for boys – they've gone beyond language, it's all diagrams, and I can't follow them. There'll be massacres down there, down in the village, if they go there a-roistering – maybe they should make do with goats, but why the fuck should I pimp for them?'

I'm quite disappointed, and to stir the air, I run down from the peak, I screech and run until the slope takes over and drives my legs, I'm like a cart without a mule, careening down, the olives whanging off like musket balls, my hair is full of vine leaves, branches gouge, I race on down, the broccoli is like green cones, I trample, smash the squashes, off the sheep scamper and the white dogs with them, now I'm in the tulips and camelias, wild onions – down go the cages for the hares, some dead in baskets, one foot clears the stream, and here's the Roman bridge that's buried to its arch in gravel, over or under it – all the same – scratch! through the bougainvillea, think of the slaves and stinking ships – and on I run, the mystery is far behind, the wise men, those philosophers, they lie in bed and think of dirty things.

Well, here's the village. Better ignorant than pacified, I think – they wanted to be slaves, to come and minister to all my wise and powerful men. No deal, those hemispheres won't meet, not if I can help.

It's ritual – I'm the bad luck boulder rolling down the hill. I'm in the village, though these guys, these villagers, aren't shades, aren't in the future they'll not live in, but they think they're getting there. I bound down among them, come to rest.

*

Here's a loafer, wants to crash up there, my crocus bulb, and

'No!' I say, 'It looks to me that you're an idle type – I'll take your wise words, but won't pay you for them, and besides, if you've no cash, you're like the rest of us. The end of life, let's call it death – gives no epiphany, each moment is your first or last, there's nothing been accumulated – it's just tick and tock. The same for you – a ball shot up and pinging down the board, the pinball game that makes you think you'll not end in the gutter! What's your name?'

'I'll let you call me Gatsby, and you're right, the gutter calls, I'm nearly done. A loser, but you'll never know what I have lost, nor what you'll gain for me.'

*

Venus says, 'There's Gatsby sleeping in the hyacinth bed.'

'And there's a bandit somewhere among the rabbits.'

She says, 'You'll have to kill them, you know. Soldier! The rabbits.'

'You'll not get me doing that.'

'You're not getting me at all,' she says.

'It's not about you. And there's a saint in the artichokes. But I shan't let them in – none of them, the wastrels.'

'I'd like to see the saint,' she says.

'It's just the clothes – they show you're holy, not that you are good. To me, they're all just bums, fine when they're winning, otherwise, they're eggshells when the chick has flown.'

*

Venus is sad. Like the old goddess, not having who she wants, and so out with her caprices, shifting shapes and genders, species even. Those old gods lived in the future, that's what immortality meant, and they were us. Those old Greeks, those Romans, rulebound, died at twenty, time for a child, a virus – then, all torn up by horses. They couldn't have the action, depth, emotion – so the goddess did it for them, lived as we do, seems an eternity if all you live is twenty years. The one who goes for sixty, seventy – adventures, wars and stretches of eternal peace, and screwing lots of different people, rejected often – it must have seemed an epic infinite, a growing, sprouting, waning, changing shape and colour, born out of shells and bulbs and heads of father gods.

'Venus,' I say, 'You want someone you can't have.'

'It happens. Often.'

'It sure does.'

Gatsby's at the window, doesn't want to enter, just attention.

The guy I call a saint is waiting for his moment. Prepared, but, you never know – he has to die in sanctity, with witnesses.

'It doesn't always happen so,' I say. You have to be prepared.

*

I've never seen her naked. I'll never see her naked. Nor know who it is she wants. Well, I'm not bothered about that.

*

It's no reward, that walking around blue land with the others gone, the humans suicided, by inertia, bad luck, stubbornness – maybe they've not just gone, but faded, been diluted. Just us two, angry, walking like the weightless.

*

The bandit tells me, 'Those of us not saints – you reach the end, but you'll have played off good luck and bad, and must have won some – so, there is a balance, justice,' and he strokes the rabbit, but it doesn't trust.

Well, if the old gods are like us, we're like them. That doesn't take philosophy! Inconstant masters, full of japes and murder, wayward, ungrounded curiosity, intellects as sharp as flints, vendetta like a club – avoid them if you can.

*

The architect's Mongolian – I said, 'No yurt, a crocus,' and he muttered 'That's banal.'

He said, 'Yurts I don't do, never seen one in California,' but for sure that isn't true – they play you tricks, these guys, these architects – no toilets, or they leave the roof off, and it rains inside like no yurt's ever done. Those elegantly thrusting crocus shoots – he copied them from potatoes, or worse still.

*

More 'powerful of the earth', this lot is keen on women, and the guy we use, he brings a cartload, some are spares, and some come from the farms around the village and say 'hi!', he hands them out like caramels.

I say, 'No shouting and no car alarms,' and some guy from up North says he doesn't shout. I say, 'Maybe you should. I've seen the future and there's no one there, I've walked around, it's land of shades and lengths of gelatine—'

'That's hypothesis,' he interrupts, 'we do our best.'

'You suicided all of us,' I shout and then I think, if that's the destiny, you shrug it off and start again, or maybe not, and while they sleep I take the tyres and wheels off some fine car and swap them for the broken ones from Venus's – her Lapsus or some such, an ugly thing.

*

Later, she drives it like it's ice cream, and we cruise through the village like we're royals, the folk are mustered on the street to mutter at us, some kids throw rocks, and so I say, 'Let me.'

I drive, and soon we're doing treble figures, sliding along, and then – is that a bunch of leaves, a bush – oh no, some lady's picked it up, she looks reproachful – it's a hen, now dead, and so – that's life. You'd planned omelettes and instead it's scrambled chicken, off we scoot, and first I want to get away, and when that's done we'll think of where to go, and if it must be with each other.

We stop to sleep, the room is doing well for bugs, they're doing roundelays and skipping high. The guy that rents the space out says, 'The lovebird suite is this. If you prefer, I've quite a decent bathroom floor, the guy in there gets up at four, he's blind and wouldn't even notice you', and so I think the bed shared with Venus can't be all that bad, but 'Yes it is', she says, then

'OK, let's get this sex bit over with, then you'll forget it,' and I say,

'Get off! Get off!' she thinks it's for that chicken that I'm shaken up, but no, I prefer a raw emotion, not having what I want is better than the having, being disappointed, or to have a plan for second times, with boredom drawing closer – though I must say, and snigger at the thought, not every guy turns down a night in bed with Venus, but that's the way I am, and Venus says, 'And so fuck you! You're finicky.'

Next morning, off we drive, we're in sour spirits, we're punished with the insects and their song all night. The blind man in the bathroom, didn't open for me, handicap or malice.

Venus says, 'It's just you, it's chicken dreams.'

I say, 'The parts – they have no sum. Add this to that – it doesn't go, there's just discrete and irreducible bits. It doesn't yield to multiplication or addition. Everything is what it is – the old prof said. Indeed.'

'He didn't say,' says Venus. 'He asked.'

'Well, we can tell him, the future's thinner than the past, we've walked in it, it's fading, and in a while we shan't be there. Especially you.'

*

We round a bend, we've not come far – and there's the crocus, as we watch, one side deflates, another flowers with flame, the shoots spout smoke, like it was a witch's hut.

Who would do that? The bandit or the saint, maybe the holy loafer, or all three – they're quite a careless bunch, or yet again, some banker or a president, maybe a king or queen, a frolicking in bed, some trick with a cigar

– and up it goes. I see the headlines now – 'The Crocus Croaks.'

At least the money wasn't mine.

We gaze, it's like Valhallah closing shop. It isn't home to Venus, but she'll feel concern.

I say, 'We should have stayed away, apart. The village went on well when choices were between the pea, the broccolo, radish red or white, and the mysterious artichoke – then we came in, not bringing things but promising as if we would, and now it's wrecked.'

I let my mouth hang open. There is silence. I wonder – and the thought flits through me like a pirate moth, bearing a skull and crossbones:

'Did Venus set it off, the fire, there's many motives for burning down your home,' but she is silent, so I ask, to change the subject, move my suspicion further off,

'Where did you say your father gets his cash?'

'I told you. Imports some ragged people, steals their earnings.'

'I thought it was a joke,' I say.

She laughs and says, 'If you find it funny, what difference does it make?'

II

'I think that Mongolian burnt it down himself,' says Venus.

'No one burns down their yurt,' I say, but of course it wasn't his.

'I thought you'd like the trick,' Venus says, 'that's theory, that's philosophy. And the insurance ...'

Ah. The insurance.

'The villagers say it was a monument,' she goes on. 'They want cash.'

'It wasn't for them,' I say.

'A church, a mosque, a monastery,' she insists, 'it was a Mystery, and so is valuable.'

'That keyless door,' I say, 'that film, meniscus, that divides us from the future ...'

'And from the past,' she adds eagerly.

'That place we go to together,' I go on, 'where there's no more atrocity, the last horror's done, and where there's no one left to ask, nor guess, nor spin a tale ...'

She stares at me and says, 'Why bother about atrocity – you know what sets them off, just think of spinning discs just circling round, you turn your back and there you are! a piece of offal on the floor.'

'It's true,' I say, 'Those discs are goddam sharp. You think there's no return, but there it is, eternally recurring. What to stave it off, the butchery? Insurance, you could try – better if your cat's not black, better not shout too loud, or hand out tractors to the feisty peasants. Destroy, destroy, or be destroyed!'

I go on eloquently, and think, goddam that thought about insurance, though in any case the acts of gods and saints are not included – full as they are of wilfulness, revenge, the whole, the bottomless, bag...

'We're in a soap of infinite dimensions, washing clean the episode before. So little learned – we even forget to insure the structures so that when they're gone, you get some cash to build another.'

Venus stares: 'You didn't forget?'

I say, 'It's time to ask your father, eternal patience hovering there above – more cash, another fortune, please.'

She's haughty: 'My father gave you money to invest, invest for me, not spend on your relentless talk, and a structure on a hill.'

I say, 'I've not the time to tell him what banking is – tell him to read a book. Love is all around us, he should be resigned – that way he avoids potential blackmail.'

She says, 'He says too, you're talking against the Turks.'

'Nothing at all against the Turks,' I say, 'forget the graves and that – every nation you can name, they've all done something bad and something for the arts, and as for schemes of government, they've all had upstart princes, drunken kings, and wills of all and saving from yourselves, and had to cope somehow with that. As for the Turks, forget the bad side, think of schemes they had for keeping guys together, untidy parcel, that's for sure, but genius – so let him read another book. Not everyone can have a state, and stamps, and what is ethnic difference, it doesn't mean a thing, you're free to screw your neighbour, in the bed or on the bourse, and that is that, the "everything that is", and may you be content with all you need.'

Venus says, 'My father expected much more than that – some fine effects, fireworks of blue and silver, things Tibetans do with sand, and operas! lots of those, the classic kind, with thunder, possibly with dragons.'

I say, 'He is a man of taste – he'll keep the waiters busy bringing wines – but what we need is money – love is free and unadorned, though not without its pricks, but that's familiar: what we need – is capital.'

'He has some Turkish friends,' she says, 'it seems, they do the deals from East and West – they're sensitive,' and I say, 'Good! For sensibility will always trump mere sense,' and I can hope.

It's not about Turks – it's about reprisals, and punishment.

III

'He wants it all back,' she says, 'And this time, it's all for me.'

'He really should read that book. What's his "or else"?'

'You get to meet the Turks. And while we're on this phobia – this stuff about atrocities – you know that it's the price of where we are, our motor. Get over it! It's slippery, this planet, and we come clothed in silks and armour, paintbrush in one hand, club in the other. These warriors are your mates. You have no choice. You stick with them.'

'Yes,' I say, 'It's *Weltschmerz*, this phobia. Wanting otherness, something different – the something else you, with that name, should promise,' though it's not her I want, it's wanting her. The Turks don't enter here – they are the past, the mirror-image of ourselves.

'I do just what I like,' she says, 'with whosoever, no one but me is keeping score. Take the cash, and double it, or else. Turks.'

IV

'This is fine stuff,' I say, caressing the travertine. Some bits of staircase, basalt probably, had come from Roman columns, there were parts of stovepipe, maybe some urns and amphorae, all blended in like brawn. On the walls, prelates in frames, long noses, don't look at us. A tall monsignor whisks past, and Venus stares, as he parades, all buttoned up.

We're looking for investment, and 'How much have you got?' a plump guy asks.

I say, 'We're looking for the opportunity, so of course we don't have any cash.'

'And if you did, how much? How much you haven't got?'

I name a sum that could build Persepolis twice over; he doesn't twitch.

'We might all be interested in that,' he says, and calls a minister, or maybe it's a priest. The plump guy asks the other, 'The stuff I sent – was active? Did it please?' – it could be drugs or arms, women or boys, or everything, a whole economy of round things, could be pills, bottoms, bullets, keels to be laid or lied about. The priest or minister laughs, 'Wow! That figure takes you to the top' – he waves his head towards the palace opposite. 'The big chief needs to know, he's loaded so he doesn't care, but likes to see his friends are doing well and getting what they need.'

I say to Venus, 'It's your country, so you understand.'

'It's yours as well,' she says.

'I'd like to take that Corvette out, you'd need some spades,' I say.

'You can't,' she replies, 'it isn't armoured – you should know these things, with being mafia, army, all your story.'

'It all means running to and fro,' I say, and think I might just try the music, now I'll owe – if all goes well – two fortunes.

'You'll never go to jail,' she says. 'They're full. It's trials that wear you down, the years you spend with judges, reading all their stuff. Waiting. You have to live forever, but it's so banal, and in the end – for end there'll have to be – a mausoleum, or unmarked grave or acid vat. Name forgotten, all of that.'

I say, 'I thought this was another source – the bankers swarm around the Vatican, there must be something here that's not your father, some pot of sweetness where there is no light.'

She says, 'The money's always round, you know. My father's in this circle too. You have to find another way...'

I think. Of course! Look at St Peter's Square – the colonnade's all skewed, for when they knocked the houses down to make the road, they couldn't change perspective, so that when you look from high – the square, the road together – there's a keyhole shape.

Beneath the Square, the keyhole shape, the clue – down there are catacombs. Maybe in use, and not to be disturbed.

'Just corpses,' Venus says, 'No money there,' but I have found the mystery – a secret from way back – some victims of the schisms, mass graves, bishops and way up, the settling of scores, a militant theology, the gods about to come with spades to raise the dead, an interesting time, basilica gets built to cover up the crime. You spill your bean, or write a book – who knows, the church is mighty quarrelsome, it wants you to obey, not to be good. And so, just like the other forces here, if you dissent – you disappear!

Venus says, 'So the secret lets you in – to maybe where you don't want to go.'

But I am fired – 'The plan is this,' I whisper on, 'Goodbye to celibacy, lots of trouble there, no profit, all those singles living out dull lives or maybe worse – that old rule, that once intrigued the rural folk – it's dead and gone. They want to build! New blood, down with the old. Here come hotels, casinos, brothels for all tastes, and sports fields for the young and fearful or the feisty on the

terraces – all males, so far, but truck them in by
thousands.'

'Tell me,' she says, weary but alarmed.

'Priests. New priests. Theology is rules, it's not
interpretation, that's what they always say. And so, you
bend the rule – and in comes luxury! Think of the
contracts, all the land, cement, machines for muscles and
for races, cellars and restaurants, cops and bodyguards!
The spending, Venus! Adonis priests. Celebrities, like
footballers – what we all want to be. Young and desired –
enough with pederasty, the gayness under wraps – and on
with girlfriends, electronic coupling, think of the gossip,
they're the gladiators, sporty types. Beautiful and strong.
When other males are flaccid, they'll be trained and
ready, guard dogs of the faith. Excess and rituals.
Concerts, blogs. Depilation. Gel.'

But Venus sulks, 'It doesn't seem my thing. Maybe
my thing won't come. That praying in the open – turns
me off. It's rather grim. Just numbers, global numbers –
all those flash boys – millions will flock: Adonis priests –
it takes the bloom right off.'

Now for my fortune – the mystery unveiled can wait.
The plump guy's got his friends a-mustered, and they're
chatting, some in here, and some are shouting out the
windows, I see a judge or two, police, and spies and
journalists.

'They think you are my father's agent, not his debtor,' Venus says, and she looks sour, but this is how the motor works, and there's no talk of roadkill, compensation, chickens, all that stuff, nor fires, insurance, deaths contrived or just in passing – the game lies in the drive, the driving on, the puffing up where there's no breath or breeze. And we're all friends, the great ship moves, the slaves are at the oars, the cash is here, we're powering on, and sex is starting up again, and horses, baccarat – here come the Brazilians, they're a laugh – and off we go, we run, and if we fall, it's lawyers and our alibis and being in the news, just like cartoons, and no one cares, and on the scene there storms another crew, all school friends too, maybe a little homosex, and sniffing here and snorting on the street with guys that love you, and you like them too, except they've got no cash, and being rough you find them tough guy stuff to do – we've all got pals who're cops and magistrates, though in the nighttime maybe they will come for you and beat you, tape your face, stuff you can't get off ...

I say, 'Here it starts. Maybe I've seen the end.'

Venus – she's lost her laughter: – religion takes off again, but not for her, no veneration now. I hardly know her, just addicted to her. She's aloof from all these guys, they fall about with naughtiness, so full of life, and wonder how to spend – when you're above a certain sum, it isn't anything, not gold, nor even plastic, just big blocks of notes, makes you forget which house you bought to stash them in, so buy some more, an island, that will do, a city and its counsellors, region and parties, nothing is too good or dear – makes you forget how much it's possible to eat or screw or shout and bring the people in, politicos – they're easy hooked, and then the whores, the priests, the men of order and of punishment – all tumble in, without a second thought, life bubbles up, not humanists or cautious, there to stay but not to last, suck it all in and wait to have it taken by another gang, go down – no, up! not save the planet but to screw it, screw until it squeaks, fun is to hear it squeak again, and don't ask why and on and on. But Venus doesn't seem impressed, maybe has seen it done too many times before – and does she miss her love, or is her lover somewhere else, untouchable, with maybe someone less ambitious but he fancies more – or is it she, who won't commit – I really cannot tell

'I'm not averse to low life,' she says.

'It sounds quite prim to say like that,' I say.

She stares round and says, 'Here comes another fortune for you – but for me, I'll make myself the centre, have some fun, but in my way. Tired of being forced, and all those goddam sisters, old tales.'

'Turks too,' I say, 'but their trade's mostly arms.'

She shrieks a little and says, 'Enough, you make me vomit,' and that closes off the scene. But I have run a course with guys like these, and when they dress you as a soldier, the rules are yours to break. Here, there's lots of rules, but they're not worth a spit.

Venus says, 'Music is better,' and I think – these guys have some ladder, kind of rope, that lifts them to the future, call it Family, great chain of being.

'No place here for me,' Venus says.

The monsignor strides back, goes up the stair, taller than ever, muttering, 'Ave Maria, who was she?'

I tell her, 'It's Schubert, he's the problem here, they think it's all about some girl next door, some Mary – they're all suspicious about music, tunes and words especially.'

'No place for me here,' she says.

I say, 'I think we're going to lose this second fortune, if these guys are handling it. I'd sooner deal directly with the Turks.'

'It's only play,' Venus says, 'it's paper cash, like some guys print it for the dead when they go up to hell – but burn it first.'

'This fortune stuff,' I say angrily, 'divination with the chickens, I don't like any of it, it all seems a scam.'

She's sad again and says, 'They're only chickens. Like the one you sacrificed. I don't object.'

I say, 'Maybe you should object.'

V

'Of course, the gesture's magnificent, the message flamboyant, and transparent,' I say.

'And one is remembered – at once. Will there be a reassemblage?' Venus asks.

The artist's body, some of it, lies on a wooden table. Guy with a cleaver chops off the parts required as sold – the head, it seems, must go for whole, the clients steer away from what the gallery people call the lower back, the fount of youth. The embalming looks, for now, secure. The saints got chopped and multiplied, and sent all over – Lenin was the lucky one, he stayed entire, integral as a holiday treat, a catacomb of one. It's true that statues come to lack some bits, but what is lost is useless, whilst this guy is all for sale.

I say to Venus, 'I love to be a patron – now we've got another fortune. I've done my best for architecture. What a fine way, now, the artist passing on to future connoisseurs – yes! no more a portrait of the artist, but a middle finger, a cold shoulder,' and I ask, 'How do you display? I'm thinking of the cats or dogs – a place upon the mantel seems a hazard,' and the nymph who oversees is firm: 'Encased, maybe in crystal, and a golden frame, which we can do for you as well.'

I hear her mutter to a colleague, 'And of course the proceeds pay his taxes,' and Venus says that souls are everything, and not for sale, so where's the harm – but we don't buy, being we two, deep down, a pair of fogeys in the aesthetic sense, fixated on whole bodies and on interior design, that far outpost of things in art, and not the least expensive.

*

The second lot of cash comes from her father. Sadly, he winks at it, 'Poor people, very poor and desperate people, had better watch out!'

'How so?' I ask.

'We fight our wars in their lands now,' he says, 'It got too dangerous for us to do explosions close to home. The minor stuff, the arms, but not the legs, haha, we sell or give – and if you don't like the bangs and bongs, then leave. There's things that they, from the periphery, can do for us – they make inventions, watch machines, and sweep the floors, look after gran, and then, there's artichokes.'

'What and why?'

'Someone must pick them or they'd rot. You like artichokes?'

Venus shrugs and says, 'There's always been crusades. They made a mess of Troy and then the Turks came in and now it's Arabs take the fall—'

'Well, let them come to us!' her dad breaks in. 'If you don't like your scrabble life, then leave! Buy a ticket, pay some guy, and come and be a millionaire!'

I don't object, it's academic, and if you don't leave the dead and dying lie, they'll stink you out. Men love seeing enterprise and putting on a show, and women too are not averse, for no one likes a loser, but his words, so bluntly put, that seem jejune and infantile, may go against the species plan. Concern for others isn't part. Ever more vertical we stand, so what we're standing on recedes, we're like great towers, worry about foundations, but our heads are well above the clouds – there the beauty lives, not in what goes on upon the ground, and Venus says, 'I'm glad I'm tall, I love the shorties, yes I do – but not as much.'

We have no time for contests about height. The Corvette's in its grave, and as we leave, I ask her, 'How can we spend this money – and still have profits, huge ones?' Now we're in cahoots, I've ceased to rob her, she's my partner now – and that is life, is how it goes.

*

'I can't believe you went soldiering,' says Venus. 'Not knowing who or why you're off to zap. Disgusting.'

'There's grading – everyone can get some job, it's easier than exams. Besides, my theory is, in every band of humans there will be a scum on top that gives the order – dregs beneath – and in between, the rest, unhappy, drawn along. A revolution wants to skim the scum and free the dregs – though dregs and scum, they need each other! Now, we have dregs and scum together indistinguishable, and on the top there's froth. And in between, the guys that bend before the wind – excuse my metaphors, but that is life. An army now ...' I pause, I'm lost. No words will come, no words will do, and then, 'An army is the stick that whirls the whole lot up, makes vortices and puts the air – right down, it mixes scum and dregs ...'

'Why would you want to be part of that?' she asks.

'Excitement, duty, nothing else to do, bring order, morality, that stuff, – by using opposites: breaking taboos, not getting caught or punished.'

'It sounds like lots of fun,' she says.

'An army's not resistance, "seven for the faith", or things like that – it's "change in uniform" ...' she says, 'stirring it all up.'

'The old prof asked – why's it all as it is?' I say, 'Well, what is, it usually just flakes off and disappears – but with the whole world under arms, with Armageddon bombs and such – wow! there's your instrument of change!'

She sniffs.

I ask, 'So, where do you stand, – not on the side of love, for sure.'

'Not love,' she says. 'Love fades. Desire goes on forever. Sex is a difference endlessly repeated, always the same – though sometimes duller or more nasty. Desire – that's the hard flame, hotter, brighter than the jewels that I don't want. Those are bits of old rock, yes, they go on and on, lifeless, but – desire is what I have and what I want.'

'The hunt! The storm! That's what I want too,' I say.

'You wanting something doesn't bring you close to me,' she says, and back we go – to where to put our money, double it, avoid the Turks, and still have some for dressing up.

'The only way to bring this off,' I say, 'is not by making things, or having guys or gals to go down mines or off in ships, still less to do all that ourselves. Go to the source! The mint! We find the place that coins and prints, and get a hold on that. Forget circulation, the hopping on and dropping off and maybe grab a bag of cash. We'd start where fortune starts,'

'Your economics stuff is crap,' Venus says, 'and factories, museums, all that stuff is out, it's all dead stock, it's things in boxes, love in family packs with sell-by dates. Tap into eternity – that's the paying deal for sure.'

And now that is my test.

VI

The dome is immense. At its apex there's no lantern, it goes on, rising, dipping, ledge to ledge. Painted like sand, the umber's flaking off, it's blue beneath. The floor is far below.

The – what is he, guru, satan, leader, challenger? – says, 'You climb across.'

I say, 'It's quite impossible.'

'That's how it looks, but,' he gestures across towards a bunch of lads far down, chattering, 'They've all done it, or done something else.'

'I'm terrified of heights. That's why I was a soldier. On the ground, with feet well covered.'

'Really a soldier?' he asks.

'I did the tests – the "shooting guys that you don't know", "defending guys that think you're wrong". I said, "Modernity's a wondrous thing – tradition too, in its right place." The complicated stuff, I'd overcome. So, when the moment came, I didn't sign. But soldier? Yes, I'd passed the test.'

'Right, then,' he says, 'this dome, you see, has little hoops set in across the surface. You must creep from here to over there, a little like an insect, cockroach, caterpillar – the choice is yours. You'll never do it dangling down, your arms will give. You put your arms like this,' and he shows, 'Then draw your legs up, move your arms along, and so you rest and push and swim.'

He pauses, and I say, 'It's quite impossible, we're not joined up like that. Those hoops, they spoil it, that expanse – it could be desert, could be sky, and if you fall...'

'You're a cracked vase,' he laughs, 'We'll glue you up and put you on the highest shelf, no one will see you're crazed,' and he doubles up with laughing, like an insect, supple as a yard of twine.

'It's too far down. And what's the prize?'

'You win my trust by winning your own faith – something will bear you up. That something is your power.'

'It's not enough,' I say, but his tongue is quick.

He says, 'It's not the fear of falling that impedes you – it's desire. You want to fall, that's it, to prove some law, to pass what's quite another test – eternal life! Yes, eternity's without time, so – the minute that you drop – that's your eternity, before eternal peace. You want to fail my test, find it impossible, and win your own. But yours is death – mine, strength and life.'

'Well, put like that,' I say, though unconvinced, 'I can't refuse,' and so I'm here, up on a ledge, the other side is arched away. I have a strategy or two, I think.

The other shore. Imagine. Below's no distance, just a warm and brothy sea, the monsters and the fish are floating round, quite unconcerned, like figures on a bowl, they've horns and hands, maybe a mermaid even, and salt galore to raise you up and give a savour to the soup ... or, maybe, falling from our poisoned rock on to another, fresh and green, where gravity's suspended, so you land like eagles homing to their nest: a flap, an eagle eye around, and home again, where up and down are much the same, and,

'Swallows think nothing of it,' the guy, the tester says.

'They've no imagination – look at those small heads,' I say. 'They don't know what it's like to bump into your friends, your brothers.'

'Get on with it,' he says, 'there's too much shally,' and I put my arm into the first hoop.

My breath is solid, can't move it out my lungs, my hands, my arms – the acid's on the boil, and this is just the first. The sea imagined just beneath, is warm; the sky is sand, you crawl upon it, sun hot on belly – then – wait! The fancy fails, it's death below, already it is summoning, – ended, all those fine schemes, the sporty cars, moments of intimacy, museums full of stuff dug up or pocketed – not worth a spit – and then I think, 'The first hoop's like the second, from first to last, your fate's the same,' and so, of course, I'm on my back, I see the sand, the blue beneath, the spots of oil or soot, insects maybe, I can't look down, I'm upside up, I hear the shout, 'Your legs – the cockroach! Creep, you monster,' and I do.

The second's like the first, my acid's coming off in steam, my legs are not joined up – I move them and they push me down, they push me off, the guru says, he shouts, 'You can't come back, there's no way back, go on and improvise.'

There's twenty hoops at least, or thirty, and my legs won't bend, they push me down, my knee comes past my chin, my ear, I hear some chatter from the floor.

I shout, 'I'm concentrating, make those guys keep quiet,' but laughter comes, they're making bets, I think they're trying to distract. I do a second hoop, I splay my legs out, they can take some weight, the journey is still perilous, I do another hoop, I'm dead but on my body goes, it crawls so slow, and yet some speed's the thing. I'm dangling here and creep so cautious, like a thing that's roused but still asleep and predators around – but now, the only predator is me, I'm fighting mind on body, mind has lost, it's all technique of bending body where it shouldn't go.

'That's the third hoop,' I hear him shout, but muscles now are full of insect blood, and on I go, it's fancy, for the me I was, it couldn't go, and now this crawling thing is powering through the hoops – at the top there is no lantern, nothing to pause with, no point in looking down, the arch below is bent like glass, the floor is tilting – yes, he's exact, the will to fall is strong, to get it ended, over, glimpse of eternity, a fine scream would do, probably you've never screamed so loud since you were born, it's quite a primal one, unconscious, no particular note, should put it in my music, and the sandy curve goes down. I'm stuck here, gravity inverted, the arch goes down, the floor is up. And yet, it's only relative, I say the arch is down, but really down is down, down there ... another hoop, maybe the hoops are rusted through, and how were they nailed up, another fear, the hoop I'm on is loose, I'm stuck, my head's now pointing down, there's no relief, my legs are lighter but the weight is back upon my arms, there's no blood left, it's going nowhere, it's all gone, burned off. I hear,

'Don't linger! On you go! Maybe you'll do it, and if not – the shortest trip you'll ever take,' and on I go, another hoop.

I'm there. The other shore. The sea recedes, the floor is back down there, tiles all squared off, I've done the trip and now, 'How do I get down?' I scream.

'The stair is over here,' he shouts, and laughs. 'There and back, it's logical, you come back to the start and cancel out the tricky part,' and laughs again.

It was a joke. You climb back up and over – through a fissure in the wall. You pass from concave creep to convex, legs are not too good, and so it ends, you're through, the test is passed, and everything is as it was, at least you know why everything is as it is, it is because you've done a thing impossible, and all set up, with hoops that's hammered in, and who knows how, some cockroach with a hammer and an alphabet of hoops, crawling on nothing, banging them in.

'Well, well,' he says, 'I've never seen that done.'

And so I shout, 'You said those kids down there had done it.'

'Or something similar,' he says, 'in their case, something not impossible, like yours.'

Well, now I've done it, I don't need to satisfy this guy. I've done a thing impossible, and so – on to the next, and no more search for gurus and the faith – the sand, the mosque-blue dome, the friendly sea, quite warm and close, but all in fancy, all in your frightened head.

'You creep!' I say.

He laughs and says, 'Your creeping and your crawling – beautiful to watch,' and I stamp off.

Venus is impressed. She says, 'Are you saying a woman couldn't do it?'

'It's impossible. Anyone could do it.'

She says, 'Everyone does impossible things these days
– running, jumping, climbing – spidery little guys, guys
with sticky gecko feet – besides, I bet you fantasised.
Pretended there was no distance down!'

'Maybe that's true.'

'So! You slither like a cockroach – and for what? Not
to impress, I'm sure.'

'Extinguishing that will to fall, that is enough.'

'Ah, desire,' she says. 'Now, that's talking sense.'

*

Some guy on TV is saying – 'People! We're beginning to
lose. So, no more torture, that's what the strong do to the
weak, it's what intelligence does to maybe knowledge.
Now, we're the ones who know, and we are victims,'
then there's the picture of some sharp fan, a thing that
rolls across the battlefield and slices, and I think that little
boys and girls must watch this stuff, and in the movies
when a guy is sliced, they do it slow and twice, so it
won't pass you by or leave some doubt or puzzle – but in
fact, when you get sliced, the better and the worse halves
fall down once and quick – no medieval romance here,
no trees as tall as heaven, gilded, knights with armour
that's undentable – a sylph, maybe, and you don't spot a
mantrap in the bushes. I think, it's normal that we think

this modern life is good as you can get and getting better, and we're smarter, quicker with the answers to questions that you've never even thought – so we'll go down, the TV says, because we haven't faith or brother love or something like, down it all goes, beneath the sand.

'Things do move on, old cockroach,' Venus says, and she's quite the friend today, though wanting some real man with something extra I've not got, and probably there's someone who'll do just as well, down in the village – though, with that desire to fall quite cancelled out, the jealousy is biting less.

*

I ask, 'Those guys, hanging around in the garden?'

'Imagination,' says Venus, Yes, imagination, like – in the village, her lover.

I say, 'I saw them before – in that eating hole, that stinks of sawdust. They ordered couscous – it's quite excellent there.'

'They must be Italians.'

'Not in a restaurant that wasn't theirs.'

She says, 'It's cover,' and she laughs at me.

We're in this misty garden, there are cachi trees, the globes like lanterns, trees without a leaf, the boughs are wet and black, the fruit so round, so orange-red. I say,

'The Turks will get us if we lose, Italians if we win the fortune.'

'You think the worst.'

I say, 'My music's going well. A trio written first, then they'll reject the big piece, chorus of five hundred, sixteen parts, but they'll imagine it – can't fit the guys and gals all in one place, and have an audience. That way, the trio wins the prize!'

Venus says, 'Of course they could. Fit them in.'

'Well, most likely they won't – and so, it's from the grandiose down a step, the prize is tiny – but the big piece – *Simplicissimus the Vagabond*! It shouts out to be musicked. The war, religion – service to the Swedish king, four devils brought to hell, there treated with some Spanish wine, the witches' dance, then – up to heaven, turned into a calf! Your eyes already full of it, your ears can't wait. The wisdom of unreasoning animals, the thievish brother of the woods – and then, apotheosis, leave the world again, become a hermit. It's the surest thing.' She waves a hand.

'So sure, it's all been done – I can't recall exactly, but you bet, the numbers follow sweetly, and it writes itself,' and she sniffs and turns, pulls down a disappointing caco fruit, she's welcome to it – that was some war, the Thirty Year one, that they said was all about religion, but it seems – just dynasties and land, all piling in, the Croats, the Swedes, rampaging, cash all lifted, spent and stolen, recoined and paid to soldiers, spent on whores and crosses, the killing and the cleansing, turning to the path of right by stab and burn and slice – 'here comes another army, well turned-out, and what the hell does this lot want?' – and on and on, the thirty years must seem enough, but not so long considering, to work it out, get ready for another one ...

Venus says, with mock concern, 'Don't get bogged in your music, you do repeat yourself, it's instructing in the obvious' – but it's all there, and not in words but shape.

'Help me! You musty novel, musicked be, and save me from the gangs. Turks if we lose, Italians if we win,' I think, and someone's been and spilt the plot and poured it all on us.

*

Lola from the couscous place comes round.

'You're quite an ascetic,' she says.

Small room, small bed, three of those cachi, Venus apples, on it.

'I got burnt out,' I say. 'Take a fruit thing if you want – to me they taste of in-between, not quite this or that.'

She says, 'I thought you were a musician – where's your piano?'

'I'm into polystylism – can't carry all that other stuff around. Besides, there's pianos everywhere, begging to be played.'

'Polystylism sounds it's for handymen.'

It's true that *Simplicissimus* is in my head, and won't take off. But I don't say. Lola maybe has the life and character I don't have, am looking for.

She says, 'I got called Lola. My parents met in a cinema.'

'Now you mention it, you look like the woman in another movie – "The End of the American Empire", something like that. Canadian.'

'Canada's a windy kind of place,' she says.

'They should have stuck to being French, for interest.'

She says, 'Poor Indians.'

We pass the bottle round. Between us.

Then she takes off her clothes. 'You look surprised,' she says, 'This is the modern way.'

'No, not at all, I thought I'd need to sugar you up,' I say, and afterwards, 'Venus says you're quite unsuitable.'

'Well, she would know,' says Lola, quite offhand. And then she says, 'You're crying.'

'No,' I say, 'just tears.'

Turks or Italians, what does she expect?

I say, 'I don't want you, I want ...' and she's not irritated, and she says, 'Honesty is best, though best for what they never say.'

*

Lola says, 'Those guys, those Italians – they said they were tuners. Pianos.'

'I don't want tuning. My pianos are prepared.'

'We had to make spaghetti. They wouldn't eat the couscous.'

*

Later, I say to Venus, 'Those gangs that follow us – maybe your father is behind them both, that way he wins, whatever comes.'

'He's not capable of that.'

I'm angry, and I shout, 'Capable? What's capable about hiring thugs?'

She says, 'Loyalty and power – that's what he wants. Repayment doesn't enter.'

*

Later still, I say to her, ' Let's see what goes on in afterland.' And there we go, through that tough skin, and there – there's always less.

I say, 'It's mostly just horizon now. A line between two blues, the shades have gone, it's just us two, no spirit here, it's going down – there's no one following here, there is no currency, maybe we don't even bleed.'

'Yes,' she says, 'They've all deserted. Even the ruins have been ruined flat, blue tarmac everywhere, and each has found their paradise, has used the last key in the bunch – and gone.'

There is no sound, no breeze, no bird, no tree to sit in if there were. Not desolation, quite, nor yet eternal peace, for we're not peaceful, bickering here.

I say to her, 'How's that guy? That you were with?' and she is startled.

'Well,' she says, 'it's not respect I'm after, like they say – rather, it's a kind of veneration, like my name, so when I've chucked them, they stay sad, devoted – visit me, but not try stalking – I've a quick way with that!'

'But there'll always be someone, someone else?'

What a fine and eager driver, jealousy!

'There always is. There always has been. But not here.'

We gaze around, but don't feel masters of the scene. The stage is empty – and no audience. No music, not the voice that comes from who knows where and must mean who knows what.

We're glad to slide right back, where we're the quarry, seeking our fortune – my Venus apples on the bed, the mattress, now there's only two. Lola must have taken one.

I ask Venus, 'Did you see the blue light?'

'There was nothing else to see.'

'Light blue by day, by night dark blue.'

'I'm for hard edge, myself,' she says decisively.

'There's no structures, just a line. Dividing equal from equal. The sun, the sun! How we miss it.'

'You can still worship it, it's there, up there, it must be,' she's mocking me.

*

'I passed the test,' I tell her, 'So there's no need for a satan.'

'What had he promised?' she asks, glumly.

'What could there be? Only vulgar things. A collection, an amassment, of beautiful things, is vulgar. One little thing is beautiful. Besides, there's every kind of satan – sceptical, a moderniser, risen, fallen – who wants more?'

John Fraser

'Well,' she says, 'That's up to us. Those mass graves beneath the Vatican – we can make something out of that – the next cull of old priests ...'

'It's re-education now, the camps are in, they'll be sent off and then – the new Adonis type. Then that will wane, they'll bring in guys that's programmers and put it all on screens,' and she follows me, irritated and bored.

She says, 'They mustn't think of monotheism, here the Romans are so happy with the saints and virgins, quite like the old time, each one has a shrine and does some miracles. Everyone's got a little fief, a kingdom with a melancholy king, a scatty queen, a princeling doped or busy with soft porn – bring in some over-arching deity, and where's the fun?'

And so, to keep her sweet, I say, 'Religion is a necessary phase – it's like the horsedrawn tram – you take the horse away, the tram goes by itself Most people can invent what they want the world to do, and what it really is. Here, it's so slow! You need some sprites and spirits frisking round, or else it's drab.'

'All this here's about the ages past!' she puts in. 'We wonder, where do people go? We walk around in blueland, there's the end, they've all gone up to paradise, or else they've melted, quite dissolved, slung in some acid bath they made themselves. It's gone, you fool, it's been determined – forget the skeletons beneath St Peter's

Square, and think! What to do now, now it's too late? We, they – we saw it coming, and it came, apocalypse, and now, what do you think to do? You've not got much, but, after all, you have your Lola.'

VII

'That hilltop,' I say, looking over at my burnt-out bulb, its bedraggled shoots pointing down and twitching, 'The Spirit came, she looked it over and she stayed, she lived there. Of course, I don't say this to folks – if you don't know it, what's the point? Maybe she lingered, now for sure she's gone.'

Venus stares at me, 'You're a sceptic – so what's this crap?'

'Don't get me wrong – I don't mean flitting fairy, looking for real estate – but there is a place, you can protect, real thing that changes with the light ...'

I lose my thread, and she pretends she doesn't understand. 'A grove upon a hill?' she mocks. 'How orientalising,' and she says to clinch it, 'Stick to your music. All those choristers.'

'Computers do it all,' I say, 'except they've no throats to clear. Perhaps I'll give each individual a part, five hundred or a thousand – why stop at sixteen, multiples? The trouble is, that out comes babble. I can get my babble free, don't need to write a note.'

She says, 'It must be very difficult now, being a composer,' and I agree:

'When you know what comes next, it makes you start from silence, like a blank, a surface – then return to it, a journey that must signify, silence at start and finish. Why not silence in between?' She's not convinced, it seems a hollow, just a pointless trudge. Perhaps she's right.

*

There's the architect! I run after him, streamers from his ankles snag in some aloes, and he falls, he's jabbering, 'Yurts is gone, all gone.'

'You clown, that was a crocus,' I shout, 'focus on the last things,' and pinned by the ridiculous, we laugh.

Calmly, I say, 'No need to burn the hocus-crocus, nor the yurt – just think, they're fields of cultural production,' and he says, 'Well, now your field's a hill – produce just what you want,' we pause, he says, 'To keep you safe, you just abstain from making fortunes, that way you're not an object of desire.'

It's true. If I am poor, no one will harm me, and I tell the Mongolian so.

He laughs some more – how good they are at laughing, these Mongolians, though at home, there's not too much that's funny, and he looks me in the eye, and says, 'You are a fool, though not a holy one. The world of fleeting spirits, here in a ruin, there a cane brake – in that world, I tell you, there's no crime, no punishment. There's maybe trials and tests, but that great rushing up to endings – penitence, all that, redemption stuff – it all goes up in smoke. The fire will show that what you build – it shouldn't linger on, become anomalous. It blows away. The image goes at once to memory, and there it blossoms, then it fades, and dies. It's up in smoke.'

I admire all this, a fine aesthetic, but I ask, 'Was it her father set the fire? To move her on, recover cash? If only I'd insured – he thought I would?'

But he's away, the architect, his clothes, the scarves, the jackets, shawls, felt boots and streamers all – they flop, unwind, I stop to gather them, as off he goes, he cries to all the world, 'The yurts is gone! Burn, burn, all up in smoke, our world.'

Near my bare room, there is a kiosk, I could live for years on burek, and I shall, that way no harm will come to me, and I won't have the cash it takes to harm the others.

*

The architect – Bayan – his studio, piled with drawings on birchbark.

'Up in a touch of flame,' he says proudly. Bulbs or pancakes, flagmasts like candypoles – the creative tinder waiting for its moment.

'Think me up a tent,' I say. 'Make it of airship silk, that could contain a thousand voices (maybe more), plus musicians, and a public' – costly, for mono-use, performance of a piece so massive it is unrepeatable, maybe put it in a zeppelin, then down below the humans running for their lives, and up above the instruments all trampled, violins will blaze, the parchments on the timpani can add their roar, the flames around are dancing blue, and all is black above and in the core the red, the orange, like the silks that kept the Road alive, and all those polities ...

'Flames,' says Bayan, and licks his lips.

'The final roar,' I say, 'that's how the piece will end, its once-performance – few will die, that's not the point, it's giving it a finish – even the players can be taped, an automaton conducts, bits of tin in evening dress, that's all. Enough! the twilight of the gods, or rings of flame – we'll send the whole lot whooshing up! A miracle of billows, just two candles set it off,' and on I go, and he's entranced.

'Yes, yes,' he says, 'Then on with the next,' he's throwing in his birchbark, anything to give a thrust, to creativity, destruction, build up and blast it down, and on, and on – the next great thing! At last, we're both in harmony, my brother, master. General!

*

I say to Venus, 'The money. To be laundered, or be spent?'

She says, a little tried, I feel, 'It's both, just pass it on, and do as you are told.'

I feel I have a plan – it's so banal, to think you change the cash to stuff that rots and rusts. Much better blaze the evening up, tent or balloon, to start again, to purify.

I say, 'Those criminals have no idea – to pay in cash and hide in holes, and polish guns and spy on cops – no life for me,' I add – 'nor you,' as a concession, but all around it seems the gangs know everything, our friends and families – better not to have them; slither round the corners, don't make fortunes, putting off the day when they will surely come – and there they are! you have to vote for them and bank with them ...

*

I say, 'Lola thinks this composing is a fraud. She says, "You write it, you don't hear it, where's it coming from?"'

Venus says, 'She doesn't care about the music, it's you the fraud that bothers her.'

I say, 'Suppose those guys, the Turks and the Italians – do a deal, join up? To split the fortune or the loss, reduce the gain but cut the risk?'

'It's likely. Father's like that. He wouldn't mind.'

'I'd mind, if I get beaten – for percentages as well. Suppose I make two fortunes, or I lose them both?'

She's silent. Whatever comes, she'll still be daddy's girl. His little goddess.

I say pathetically, 'I'll be working for the mafia.'

She says, 'We all are. Just enjoy what's left.'

In the blue light, her eyes are darker, flesh cold, but not mineral, not stone, as if she's frozen in a nightclub.

*

She's bored. She says 'I'm tired of making your life exciting. I'm off to break some rules.'

I think – doing what she does, the rules aren't very significant, broken or whole. She says, 'I'm off to the village – quite some adventures there.'

Lola's a simple soul who reads Pascal. Venus is twisted, like this hopeless olive tree, survivor of the fire and clinging to its rock – she never reads a book or thinks a thought that's not already in her mind. What's there, then, down in the village, fancy taken?

Once more I kick around the ruins, soggy grey, and looted: plastic chairs, two legs cocked up, nozzles for gas or water, panel that says 'Zorro', maybe a boiler or a piece of art that makes you think of Zoroaster – where was its place, I wonder? Bayan makes you think, but that is all.

*

When she returns, I tell Venus, 'Bayan thinks all creation should be consumed. By fire.' I pause, then 'I agree,' I say.

'You didn't when your crocus was going up,' she says.

'It liberated me.'

'No,' she says, 'I'm free, you're not.'

I say, 'Explain! It seems your father gives you all the cash you need.'

'Exactly.'

'Lola doesn't think like that,' I say.

'Wage slavery cooks your brain' says Venus. 'I make my own myth, no one tells me what. No one has ever told me.'

'Well,' I say, 'There was always your father. And the guys.'

'Father blunders on. He threatens. I don't.'

I say, with envy, 'You're a well set-up scene.'

She looks pleased, and says, 'I lead, you needn't follow. I'm just the object of your unfulfilled desire, I can make you dance in redhot shoes.'

I say, 'So, we're back with Bayan and his fire. He says – the quality's in lost things. You may remember – if you don't, you just invent. And there's your imagination, there's the rock where your own twisted tree takes hold, and slides a hook of root down where it can stick.'

She finishes, 'And when the olive's burnt, it's ten times lovelier, because it's fixed inside your head. How dull – I like to be out there, showing off – if you remember me, that's bad for you. Remembering, you've taken nothing from me!'

VIII

This guy is short and busy, pulling me along. 'We'll do your big piece now!' he says, and puffs himself, as if he were me – the me that he expects.

Oh no! – I have the shape, but nothing's written down – and mustn't be. Don't even know if I want the chorus, my five hundred live – or fewer Spartans – still more as demented horsemen, a thousand Garibaldini, cobbling together Italy – no! Clearly none of these. The thing is – it mustn't make a fortune – consequences are too complex now.

The guy, Sergio, slides open some big door. There they all are, five hundred, plus five hundred of the other sex or thereabouts, they wave and some say 'hi!' He's proud, this Sergio.

I'm granitic, and I say, Why'd you bring this crew together – nothing to do.

'The money's here!' he says.

The piece is not.

Her father, nature's banker – banking is all about your debt, the money once you gave them, now it's gone, bad luck.

Venus is cool, but Lola's pleased for me, for her, even for this short Sergio she's never seen before.

I say, It doesn't always happen as you think,' and wonder why the coolness of the lady's more to me than Lola's warmth.

I spend a morning wriggling away from my beating – Turks, Italians, others, camped out in the village.

Finally, I write:

IMPROVISE.

'*You are a thousand – splendid instrument each one, plus others massed behind you – brass, silver, tin and wood, and skins of animals, rare plants, and the electric ones.*

'*A hymn, a battle cry. A lament, a prayer.*

'*You're in an airy temple, you must invent the gods, the heroes, waiting for you, playing tricks – now is your chance!*

'*Release the birds, see the host arise, the songs, the claws unclenched, the dull frothing of the feathers – lift-off from the branches to the stars.*

'*Think of the lakes below them, sylphs in the clearings, nymphs in cane brakes, the roofs carnelian, the lakes – furrowing opals, eel tracks, riffs of breeze: you're rising with them, you to your paradise, they fall away as you rise higher, beyond the cliffs, the mountains and the stars, the air thins out, the song is dwindled down, and you look up – the Sun! the Sun! the start and finish of it all.*

'*And is there catastrophe up there? – you are so many, so strong and free, but – prudence! division, love deferred ... you daren't look down – but there are depths, the rocks – split. Your bodies, ah, so*

*vulnerable, that die in ditches, spoiled, all jumbled up in graves and
fever pits.*

  '*There is no end, there is no pause ...*'

*

At this point, the fire will start ... the singers, marshalled
into many parts, one counters neighbour, but I think there
is a harmony, of sorts, though it is fleeting, the instruments
bray out, and up the ladders climb the strings, and slither
down like firemen all alight.

The tent, balloon, will burn, the music should go on,
they'll sing beyond the end. And this I'll forge and polish
– I'll trust in them, and when the flames have reached the
roof, I'll sidle out, and they'll stream out as well, and
some will scream and some will cry, but in the end – All
Live! It is a kind of saving, they have seen the heavens,
flown with the birds, climbed the chimney-shapes of air,
the gyres, the spirals, feet in crevices of zero, gaining in
hope and confidence – and up they climb – that spangled
air – and no one slips or falls or fears ...

*

'Artist immolated in Fire' I read:

'This massive work – Piece – was about to start. A thousand voices – swelling to a sleepy fingling, like starlings waking. Then – the flames, the rushing and the shouting. Crackling – of scores, even of fat and flesh. The composer – sole victim.

'Now, all's deleted, no more music – though not silence – Bayan's tent, first scuds of silk and then consumed: the doves, perhaps, to figure in some climax – went up like scraps of nothing much,' and on it goes.

It could have been no better. The voices, all that piping, and the heads, turning and bobbing – couldn't understand instructions, whisper, consternation, who's to start it off, the Piece?

Now I'm dead and quite anonymous, I just slip off and dodge assassins, Venus too, who could have stopped it all, but that's her way – her lovers get it worse, the rest are not transformed, but dangle, sweat it out – perhaps one day her caprices end!

I don't exist. It's good, my body's lovelier than it was, it's purified, but not by fire – just the idea, the presence, voice. The shape was there, apocalypse – a little premature – was planned. It all came through, the sound, the screaming, uplift. Trace of loss, but mostly it's relief. The news goes on –

'Where then's the artist? – sad, but we're all right.'

The guys rolled out the timpani, no instruments abandoned, and I think – too bad the flutes, violas, didn't drop in flight, but here we are, only the tent has gone, beached airship. What a blaze! What satisfaction – and in joy, I kick my heels and click my fingers. I am Pan without his pipes, and off I go, safe, and unrecognised.

*

Venus says, '"Piece" was a lousy title. The village guys are savaging you like puppies.'

I'm not much hurt by this, I say, 'Lots of talent, small output – that is me. At least I'm free of your father and his goons.'

She says, 'Briefly. Now you're dead, we all trust you.'

Even father, Romano.

'My father has a bigger plan than yours,' she says, 'Though you're still in it. Think of the armies, marching up and down in Italy.'

'Bandits down there,' I say, 'and everywhere, and soccer fans, and in the North – secessionists, and then there's bands that come from everywhere,' and I think of *Simplicissimus*, though his were bigger armies, I suppose – and would it be an opera? ballet would be fun – there's more to look at, though in both you're quite shut out, if you can't sing and dance, up on the stage they really do it for themselves, you couldn't climb up there and join them, not to convince, and Lola says that she's quite pleased I'm virtual roast,

'Those posthumous works – those sell the best,' and there's encouragement that seldom comes, and Venus shouts,

'You guys! Remember how often you have read the prayer – "to free our country from the barbarians".'

'So, here they are again,' I say, 'and we the most barbaric – what does your father, venerable sage, boss of all bosses, propose?'

'He thinks that politicians have the better time, that though they think and do the same as criminals, there's less responsibility and loyalty – and they don't have to hide in holes.'

'Not all the time,' adds Lola, but the picture's clear, though not original.

Venus goes on, 'He has in mind a union. Of all the powers, all the real forces in our inland sea, Turks, Italians, Macedonians too, and if you want, the winner decides religion, or just leaves it as it is. The armies, bands, oppressed and not, the smugglers and the smuggled – throw them all in, together – there! There's your new order.'

Lola and I are not impressed.

'Barbarians?' I say. 'Where do they come in?'

And Lola asks, 'This new order – it's just what we have now.'

*

There's that tall monsignor again – so tall there's maybe two much shorter ones that's joined together – as he passes me, he whispers, 'Not mass graves – catacombs.'

The Square Affair, I think, and as he disappears he says, 'Not celibacy the problem – just finding beautiful young men.'

And Lola says, when he's long gone, 'And women.'

I'm surprised, but that's the way she is.

I say, 'I bet he won't be culled.'

'No,' she says, 'he'll be in charge,' and that too is the way she is.

Romano – 'Roman' when he's 'over there' – is not surprised to see me, walking, dead. It rather spoils the show, but then, the show is always his. He says, 'I want my money still,' but he has found some bigger fish.

I ask Venus, 'Why'd you let him see me?' and she pouts and turns, and that's the way she is, all air inside, magnificent and tall, but strewing malice, dropping a poisoned garland round your neck, and then farewell with misty eyes or maybe just short sight.

I wonder why her father who has everything, and also that Corvette, should want to be the boss of all, but naturally you're no one if you're not a king of kings – avoid those goddam elections, they're like you're nomad chief and have to get the clans' approval, messy banquets, drinking blood from skulls and all that macho stuff.

We each avoid the other's eye. He says, 'My daughter gets it wrong.'

She turns away again, it's not her thing at all, might mean she has to serve some food, or find a mother for herself, a wife for him, and stand around in niches with her arms upraised to send a bit of sex or chill around the room, the tent – whatever polystyle in politics may bring.

I say, 'Around this little space, this sea, you've this misty allsorts of feisty people, some oppressed and some oppressing, some with faith in X, others who call on Y to do the others down, bandits and liberals, diggers, sailors; some love the sunset, some its rise, some hunt with eagles, others favour quails,' and I continue till we're all frustrated.

Romano says, 'You're exactly why I've my idea. You talk too much, so what we want is strong guys to one side – cops and the mafia, all armed men – enough of these false wars that no one wins and no one stops. Put all the strong together – they're unstoppable – down go the rest, peace junkies, searchers after self, fast-fooders, concert goers, all the passive crew ...'

It seems I've heard it all before. I say, 'You'll have to wear a suit and tie.'

For once young Venus nods, but Lola says, 'They don't all do that,' and Roman gives us all cold eye.

'It seems to me,' I say, and I am thankful I am dead and cannot be pursued for debt, 'Beside this understandable desire to crush the weak, your victory, and slog it out along with guys that look like you – there's just a trace of mission here, of shaping. 'Order', 'new'. A sprinkling, perhaps of – Teleology?'

I pause, triumphant, but he doesn't hear, or chooses not to, then, he snorts 'Theology? No, no, there's none of that – they'll have to fight it out to see whose god or gods – or none – is best – that's not my thing,' and there I leave it, neither is it mine. I wink at Venus, with a wink that says, 'We know, we know! Blue light is how it goes,' but she ignores me, that's her way, and I'm quite glad, she is the point that doesn't turn when all else turns – it reassures.

*

Romano lectures us: his manifesto.

'In forest and in sand, we have to draw our line. Unite, and build a virtual wall. Inside, is us: all, every, sort – chewers, swallowers, stewers and roasters, seethers and fryers, red flags, black ones, white ones. Vulgar ones with lots of stripes, and outside – your barbarians.'

Well, I think, there's the barbarian problem solved, and on he goes: 'It's not just world union of bad guys. You need your good guys too, and as there aren't too many and they cost – look close to home. They're us!' and Lola smiles and Venus too, but less convinced. He goes on:

'Let's say that all the guys outside are bad, but then you make your deals to keep them in their place. And if they want to breach that wall – why, then we'll all take up our arms, we're all at one. If you don't build that wall, the world's a global gob of bands and gangs, car chases never end, the shootouts never cease – and you can understand, my dears,' and he turns a fat yellow eye on us. 'I need my sleep. Peace. To dream. Without a goddam row outside. A palace with no guards, or just the minimum. Mediterranea – we'll start with that – a good slice, that, a cake that's full of plums and roses, grit and blobs of gold. I know it's all been done before,' and he yawns, I see he loves his sleep.

Sleep, where adventures come upon you unannounced, you take a trip, or maybe screw some girl you never saw before, or sell some serfs, or save a lion – a place that's wonderful, a country, continent. He's nearly there, he's off, he's off! a part is still behind his desk, a Richelieu with loyal cats – the rest in dreamland. Here comes the transport – could it be it's that Corvette? – which is it to be, Sodom, Gomorrah, cities on the hill? The great thing about sleep, is there is always on your lips a smart and well-cooked answer, when you shake – kaleidoscope is always primed, to make another symmetry.

I say, and think kaleidoscope, 'You could make one with real jewels ...' but he's away in Empireland, the Romans are in Rome and he's the chief, they don't do work, they go to movies and to fights, each week they kill a zoo and long for more, they dream of slaves and vengeance measured out – buckets of blood, oysters at dawn. That's the life, and others dig and rake, sweat in their armour, get flogged, and cheated – yes, Romano's vision is a wonder, how could we have let it slip?

He starts up again: 'That wall – we didn't make it high enough. The other bad guys came right in, and what a nightmare. Some you convert to nothing much, praying and stuff, but generally the bad ones don't have office skills and handing round the cash – they want it all themselves. This time the virtual walls will be – so high,' and he waves his paws. 'If not – dark ages, Venus, that's what comes.'

IX

We leave him to his plans. Then Venus says, 'You think I'm idle, just a tease – well, I go deep, I'm into fashion.'

'O no!' I say, 'Cooking is good, and you can eat it if you're there on time, and other things are fanciful – needlework and building things and watching them burn down.'

'Otherwise they leak and peel,' Lola puts in, 'and what's the fun in that?'

'All kinds of things produce and slip away,' I go on, 'but give you fun in passing – but fashion! Those clothes! The body smell, and clinging round you, hot and tight.'

Venus sniffs: 'I don't dress, I drape.'

I am at full thrust, I say,

'And so, the slipping off your paunch, and when when you eat they crack apart, those goddam belts and stuff, – that when you want to throw them off, the gears all stick, the cogs are mashed, desire is up the chimney, screw with socks and hat – it isn't done, my dear,' and I am eloquent, although without our clothes – or animals that croak and give us theirs – and rendering plants and tanning works, and skins upon the door and falling off the sled 'o no, there's wolves' – I don't know what we'd do.

Now I understand why Bayan says, 'The problem is, this world's too cold, the houses too, you have to cut the lovely trees, or shiver nude,' and that is true -

I say, 'The body is an awesome sight, unclothed, vertical or horizontal, better a nicely polished stone, a leaf will do – the body shows you that things natural are not always nice.'

'You'd not complain if you saw mine,' Venus says, but even Lola, who's a willing sort, is far from the ideal, and I tell Venus – naked, I'll never see – 'Peeking at bodies you can't have? Or if you want what seems the next, the necessary step – it's not the nudity you want, but something else, where beauty, symmetry, means another thing, or often doesn't mean a thing at all.'

'Well,' says Venus, 'I do clothes. Not sex. So, accommodate yourself to that.'

*

We return to Romano and his plans.

Lola says, quite wisely, 'It's all another way of getting wars and money,' and I think, 'Those ways are same ways – though maybe those ancients, Italians, just did it as they liked. Not capitalism as the natural mode of human life, the ultimate, Thule, goal once reached that there's no going back, nor forward – but: as it comes.

The simple life of baths and slaves and phalluses on sticks and tombs like metro stations, one-lane roads – just trundle on and on – over the sea but not to Skye, and civilisation on a skewer, unfunny comedies and leather pricks and ostriches decapitated: – what a laugh!'

Venus is saying, 'Perfume...' now, that is a thought – forget the clothes, the hats, the pants, the trap to hide a pustule or a clump of hairs – perfume calls the wild, and doesn't hunt, exterminate.

'Yes!' I say, to no comment, no one, 'I'll help! I'll climb the tree, follow the bee – I'll trace the flower, the bower where musky creatures drop their essence – I'll mine the wave, locate the shell ...' and on I go, and we are stood, the three of us, like graces in a grove – we've just been told the sibyll's rhyme, the secret that will bear us – flyers without carpets – sweet-scented ambassadors – that 'perfume rocks the room'. Of course, nudity acceptable at last, but if you're scented right, an oil, some vial – you clothe the ugliness with angel dust, an unguent, cloak all-over, invisible, concealing ...

Venus says, 'We cook it all up in the lab. The natural stuff just reeks.'

A hollow perfume, that's the thing, that comes from no-man's land, postnature reigns. It's still a challenge, after all.

*

I don't tell Lola about the blue time, blue light. We don't go there together.

*

We're there, blue land. Things here are flattening out. There once were levels, layered right in History – some actors had their part and couldn't stray and improvise – but now, the President, he takes his women out, drives them around and dumps them in the fields, and some are cut up, some are worse, the deputies run guns and pimp.

'Do you remember when the worthy ones were unbelievable but good,' I say to Lola, 'the dark news always made by dregs? But now, the drama's gone, the powerful use their power, they all do what they like, go on TV to boast.'

'No,' she says, 'I don't remember when it wasn't like it is. It's good that we all do all the things we like – unless you're moralistic ...'

'Morals don't come in,' I say, 'there's just no fun, when there's no crime, no punishment, no character.'

'No,' she says, 'that means nothing to me, character is who you are,' and I desist.

John Fraser

*

To lighten up, I say, 'Let's all get drunk, and wear her clothes,' the ones that Venus spins, and think that maybe we could dig the Corvette out, but Venus says, 'You mustn't touch it, it's there special,' and she scowls at me.

They're not quite clothes and more than masks. They could come from some orgy – though sharing things is not her way.

'I want the owl,' I say, and Lola is a cockatoo, the village guy a crow, and Venus is a swan – not in good taste, I feel, but she lets me slip the flat face, stunted beak, over my head.

'No, no!' Venus says. 'The bird of wisdom must go naked' – the others swirl about in sheets and cloaks.

'Then that's enough of wisdom,' I say, 'No nakedness for me.'

Venus takes the head and says, 'No wisdom and no car. And walk in darkness. Suffer now and when it's done, you go to hell. Presumptuous!'

Lola says, to warm us up, 'Hey, Venus, you sure know how to spoil a party,' but I know we haven't taken on the spirit of the birds – these heads are not like hats, creations, – that once bore fruit and now have writing and an insult – but things that almost lived. And we are sober now, and sad, and Venus passes us her charge of sadness.

'Lola!' I say, 'She hexed me! Venus did!'

'Then hex her back.'

'I hardly think that's wise. There's the Italians after me, and then the Turks, that dog, the other day, a Bafra packet in its collar, that's a sign. The Corvette that stays buried till there's peace all round. Win or lose, someone's unhappy, and it's me. Her father doesn't know if I'm a corpse or just half dead. Then there's the Vatican, their hit squads almost never caught – then the Mediterranea scam – we heard it all before, "our sea", and then disaster. You won't know it, but that Collateral Campaign, grand scheme – the same, it ends in tears or boredom.'

'That's just in a novel. We did it at school,' says Lola.

To soothe myself, I play a little – the start of *Simplicissimus*.

'Here it comes,' I tell her, 'a structure made of wire that no one sees, and not piano wire, a structure like a fountain starting up, then falling back. It's over.' She is silent.

'Not like a picture,' I go on, irritated, 'stick it on the wall, it's there till it falls down.'

'I know that.'

I play along, I thump, I sing. I turn to her, applause is due.

'I didn't know you sang too.' she says.

'That's a crap response,' I say. 'As we're being intimate, let me just say – that sex thing. When we're there, you say those names, those names it seems at random ...'

'Yes, it's random.'

'That's what I mean. A bit more care. The job on hand. Perhaps.'

She laughs. 'If you want virgins, you have to pay.'

The blue light – there you have peace, there you're alone – in my case, you're alone with Venus, though she's hexed me, a falling-out that makes me fear – her father. Surely it can't be him, that's swept away the people, even shop assistants, nowhere to fix your car – even the glorious Corvette's stuck outside, a hippo in the mud, quite useless.

I ask Lola, 'Could Romano do it, have it done, bring the whole thing down – the wires that hold it up, incautious snips, can do it so much harm! The Montenegrins with the Syrians, Jews with atom bombs, and couscous over everything, a mash of things that want to be apart ...' and Lola laughs again.

'Old fogeys never die,' she says. 'It's all adventures, everyone has a plan, we spin along, we're still there at the end, and each one sings and covers up the one that's next and out of tune,' and I think, no, we're not together at the end, there's my unwritten Piece, where at the end there's sixty-four times sixty-four, and each one has their part, and then the fire ...

I say, 'Lola, back to sex, couldn't you?'

'It's all, it's everything – all in your head,' she trips off, laughing back, and not without affection.

122 *John Fraser*

X

'It's the easiest thing, to be pessimistic,' says Romano, and adds, not without affection, 'You zombie. Remember, service before everything!'

'I know,' I say.

We're in his jet.

The good ones, he calls them, aren't interested in domination, but in their fiefs. A consequence, he says, of elections and limited terms – or, permanence on precarious thrones. So, it's up to the bands and gangs to follow the big vision, wars and peaces. And they're eager, they're cutting deals. It's true they don't trust, and for sure it's not religions, diet, they believe: percentages maybe.

'What's that, down there?' he asks, leaning on the pilot's shoulder, like a sea eagle spotting a dead herring, peacefully afloat down where the wrinkled sea meets cliff. Can't be a galley, though it has little beetle legs, a blue against the grey-green water, skating along.

We pitch down, the pilot folded over his instruments with Romano atop and pointing, aiming down.

'Ratatatat' he shouts. We're vertical, the stuff on board and us is pressed against the windshield, and I see

– the beetle is a boat, the legs are nets or something like, the smell up here is burning clutch, we're screaming.

'Bastards!' he says. 'Traffickers, fishers of doomed species!'

Down we go, the shadow of the plane, the howl of our descent, have terrified the sailors – out and over, off they go, and in the waves they feebly splash and flee.

We don't hit. There's no rear mirror in these things, so what becomes of ship and sailors we won't know, we skim along the waves like dolphins or the flying fish the tourists love to see and eat.

'Well, that's the drama done,' he says. 'Just sit, relax,' and as I'm doing so, backsides explode ejected, up we go, the seats are lucky, down they go at once, but we hang there on parachutes like gurus coming back from trance, the little things go big again, we're down in automatic, on parade.

'I like to make a show,' Romano says.

There is a banner here, it says, 'Bad guys welcome bad guys', there's guards of honour, goons that stand in line, Romano trots by, nose to the stars, and I trot after, good dog among the wolves.

Inspection time. Here's a big loon, and I say, 'Hey, sonny, lace undone!'

As he bends, I take his shooter, wave it around, until Romano says, 'I'd not do that, even if I was you.'

'Why am I here?' I ask.

He says, 'That's what we all ask, it's what brings us all together ... You're a musician, and we guys, imperial, have always brought accompanists and poets, stuff like that – look at Nero, inventor of the violin – it's not just raw and crude we do, it's art,' and here is Bayan, maker of this conference hall – at first it seemed a lighthouse, ziggurat, or just a scribble, first crossed out, then built.

'It's a tower of the winds,' Bayan says, and fire is in his eyes.

Romano puts a long arm round him and says, 'Space and music – space and space – you two can get to pay a little off your gross, insatiable accounts.'

Bayan is used to this, to me Romano says, 'You're here to music us,' and he shows a little booth, a chair, a keyboard. 'Something like the Boyars' March to send us in, and then goodbye, in rosy spirits. We'll fly in an orchestra ...'

I think of Piece, unwritten message, but maybe three thousand voices and the instruments to match would bring unwelcome curious in, so I desist, and say, 'OK – one order or commission's very much alike if you have few,' and so the meeting starts.

The bad guys look like good guys, maybe more serious, and these chiefs don't have a lot of smaller guys to tell them what to say, and each one says just what they think or feel.

Romano says, 'There's trouble in the world today.' Some nod, some yawn, but no one interrupts. 'Our mission's to create a climate for our businesses, where each can live, compete, not get in the eye too much, but still decide, command, get work for guys, invest in peace,' and the nodding grows.

He stands with arms upraised. 'We saw the commies off!' and there's applause. 'The rest – it should be easy. Priests, and these elected guys – it all will pass, the teleology's not there – if we are smart, we'll win the day. The Word! Well, there are lots of those. The afterlife – we've all been there, or nearly, and it doesn't match what we can have right here.'

The rhetoric is mounting – some colleagues, pale from desk or maybe underground, are flushed. The first proposal comes:

'A pantheon. This religious stuff was dead a while ago. It's monotheism that's the snag – it lets interpretation in, divine intervention's nowhere seen, but still there's disputation. In the past,' he flaps his wings, 'they cooked the deal to halt the shooting, laid it down, "to each his fief, and there believe just what the boss decides". But now – we move around, we change our minds, all stuff you know about, and so – we change our

tune: call them – "your gods and goddesses", stick
pictures of them on the walls. They have a good time by
themselves, the deities, and if they intervene – it's just
for fun, so take it in good part.'

And on he goes, theology spews forth, the nods are
rhythmic, nodding off – I see that Bayan has a tent set up,
his banner says, 'O Fortuna', and a sign, 'the goddess
takes bets to win, at any time, in any currency', and that's
quite smart, there's guys inside in suits, with baskets for
the notes, a truck stands round the back and wow! it's
guarded well, I think they sacrifice the drivers when each
run is done, to stop the bad ideas, and where's the bank
that's safe enough? but no! of course, they put it into
holes, and when dug up it's off again, the cash. And cut
the bankers out, just like the people want ... and as I
muse, I hear Romano say, 'Off to imperial times! From
now on, pray for health, and money, sun, and victory –
you don't pray to, but for. And that's the human way.'

I see there is a cage, it's full of women, bobbing slow,
I think it's breaktime show, but then I see 'For Sale'. A
little market well controlled, and maybe I was wise to have
my Lola stay at home, and then Romano says, 'Another
problem's come to view. There's lots of guys unhappy
with their fate – not for the cash, as after all we handle
that – the feisty ones can always find a place. The same
with votes and rights – they'll vote for who they want, and

we're agreed, that men are men, for all that, and their women too, and little kids are useful in their place, and pricing right for everyone is what we do ...' he pauses.

'Here is my crux. This Palestine. Two lots of people who are quite alike,' and I remember how we, from Mediterranea, all kiss when we meet, and some don't shave, and some wear robes, but in the end – it's food that brings us all together, we eat each others' stuff, and kill for jealousy and make the widows dress in black – and as the customs fade, along come guys who will insist on custom and on purity, and on it goes, and weddings, funerals – all the same, all over, prayers and that, and hating, loving – possession being law ...'

He pauses again, then says, 'We think those Arabs should decide – an earthly paradise is best for them.' There is more nodding, and he plonks the word, 'Madagascar. National home.'

Then, there are days of argument, proposals come – Italians are keen to see their Naples moved – the West Sahara beckons – but then there's Sicily, and other parts, in fact it might suffice that every city be transposed to somewhere else, far, far from all the others. Then some guy says, the English are all bastards, should be sorted out according to the history they're all so keen on, go to Copenhagen, somewhere north, or off to Ireland, and the Irish too are better off elsewhere, and that brings in

America, already quite a dump and showing it, the blacks
go home and lucky them! – but no! the space is running
out. Tibet's to move, there's Kirghiz everywhere, some
goddam zones are cold and some are hot, and some are
waterless, and so – we all agree – we need more time,
and someone brings in maps and figurines, just like it's
playing soldiers, on they go! the masters of our destiny,
and soon there's fighting everywhere, the arms are going
well, and atom bombs are bad for business, but some
guys are nervous and would like to try them out. And
then Romano says – and shows that he's a statesman of
the highest kind, and pity me, that I'm in debt to him –

'Colleagues! Put those games away, we'll meet here in
another month, and make the final choices then.
Meanwhile – there's dancing in the cage, they're all for
sale, and place your bets with Lady Luck,' and there's
applause.

To me he says, 'And now, you creep – where is our
march?'

There wasn't time, and so I strum a bit, it's in five
four, the bosses stumble in and out, but some are lame
already so it doesn't show. Romano snarls, but now the
show is over.

There's one more trick, and that is Venus – she has
made a uniform for each of them, but they're all leaving,

'Next time, next time,' her father says, but she's annoyed, and he will suffer for it, like the rest of us.

Then, 'Hold it! Hold it!' here comes Venus with her van. I'll swear they had all left, and Bayan's set his fire, and up! the tower, that's made for air above and fire below, should go: destruction, that sends the money round. Now, here she comes, and less than clothes, they're costumes – each boss his own, and here's a Horus, there a Moses, or it may be Santa Multifaith, an Alexander, and who knows, a Sweeney Todd or Scarface, Bonaparte or Wallerstein, Heliogabalus or Mithra, there a druid, here a minor Buddha – bosses stand in line and put them on.

There is no bird of wisdom, that's still mine for when I feel like stripping off – and there's much babble and a questioning. I say to Venus, 'Don't you ever think of anything new?'

She is angry and says, 'From a polystylist, that's too much,' but we're quite friends again. She is magnificent, and, yes, she's draped not dressed, as if to greet her Rama, or it might be naked owls, certainly, she's classier than Lola, but she's quite fenced off. The bosses don their sheets and shrouds, they're photoed quite anonymous, in disguise with faces hidden, indescribable, and later on I see, behind the bushes, all the stuff, the heads, cast off, but Venus says, 'Well, that is life. And art.'

I guess she's planned it all that way – the goons shoot off their guns, and some fire in the woods around in case there's animals, maybe a pair of horns to stick in someone's throat, and sonny boy, who's gun I took, says he'll remember me. I tell him that my memory's fine, he's in there too, along with every spring and winter there has been, and rock and twig, and hide and seek, and winning poker hand – and we both sneer, he thinks I've made a threat. So, off we go.

*

Back to Lola. I tell her – 'There were the princes of the earth, our bit of it, and all together.' Romano. My debt.

I say, 'Who's the guy in your kitchen?'

'Just a guy. You're not jealous?'

'That's my strength,' I say.

'Just a month, you were away. So, you can call him May.'

'That's last month.'

'Well,' she says. 'There you are. Last month.'

'I don't think he's called May.'

'Well,' she giggles. 'There you are too. Aren't you lucky. And there's been someone from the Vatican. Snooping. With a halberd – in the trunk of his car.'

Go far away, think of the little melons, the Kazakhs smelling them. Hills with snow, lakes with bright fish – you catch them, they tell a tale, you let them go – but when it's time for lunch, why, there they are! on salvers, and happiness and love all round. Why did I choose to live here? What sin, what excess to be paid for – protection from the Boss, then the withdrawal: death in acid, dwindling, like a candle, pencil of bone and smear, then – nothing, just nothing. Even without this Lola, I could cry, or scream, or shoot the arrow high – that triggers off the rain of golden darts ... Get rid of them, the bosses all – the fantasy you mustn't have, besides, it's useless and forbidden.

I say to Lola, 'Words don't help.'

'That's good, that's right. But love there is, it bubbles on the stove,' and I say, 'My hunger's gone. It bubbles till the vessel's dry.'

'Life has rules too, you know – the causal chain.'

I must make my Piece. Alone.

*

'No more blue time for you,' says Venus. 'You're quite my father's dog, or maybe fox... Yes, Mister Tod, or Master Death,' and she swoops away. Romano says to me,

'There's trouble with my plan. This moving populations – when we have a solid group of gangs, of clans, yes, we can threaten. People move, and so a problem's solved. Yet that big idea I have, is make the good guys, as you call them, with their reason and their plans – administer the ones we shift! So, they move, because their life's removed and set up somewhere else. The documents, the mailmen, methane if you have it – it's all moved, quite quietly, no one's hurt – it's just that what you do today in Ethiopia or in Tuva – tomorrow you will do the same, in Tuva or in Ethiopia. It's such a little thing, it's the giant step we could never make, us humankind. We scattered out upon the earth, and then the prophets and the stuff to sell – all ended up in what they call the conflict zones. So, this giant step is just the second step that puts things right. Peace – and I'm the one that makes it. Otherwise, it's just a league of bad guys stepping outside of their trade. Settling disputes is not their thing. En masse – you need the good guys, they're the oil, the incense – turn the wheels and grease the rails.'

I say, 'I grasp the difficulty – although, as boss of bosses, you should be as potent as a king of kings – that's not so bad.'

'You cretin!' he shouts at me. 'It's not for me! It's the Idea. And Venus too – desire for what you can't imagine, so can't have. She's in there somewhere.'

'Maybe if you drove the Corvette ...' I think, but here's dilemma, with my debt and many threats, I can't afford belittling the guy.

*

Later, a message comes for me. 'Award! Composer with the greatest promise of the year',

'Your promises have topped the others,' Lola says, but it's jealousy, with Venus ever worse.

'What's this prize worth?' I ask.

'Well, really nothing,' Lola says. 'It's a commission – a new work. More promises,' and she laughs.

It could be the Piece reworked, or *Simplicissimus*.

I ask, 'And who's to do it, when it's done?'

She reads it out. 'The cross should be between Italian and Turkish idioms ...' and on and so.

I see the point, and say, 'Romano got me the award,' and there is laughter all around.

My backside aches from that huge kick that got us parachuting down – and then I say, 'Oh no – I'm dead, but then, Romano knows I'm not, or only half, and resurrecting when I serve, it hasn't helped at all.'

'Eternal art is never dead,' Venus laughs too when she hears. 'That's why it isn't like your life at all, nor anyone's. Besides, remember, "Welcome Bad Guys" – there were lots of dead like you. That death is quite like immortality, you're present when invoked, and when you're not, you're just a name.'

I tell Venus, 'Those projects your father puts about – they're rubbish. He's into Africa, Ethiopia, then Tuva, who knows why.'

She says, 'I expect he knows they're rubbish. But the longer sight, it's *cultura italica*, don't you know?'

'Maybe your mother should have told him?' – I angle for this, her, answer, exactly,

'Mother took off, she went abroad, back to where ... and left me with this name, and this alone. Divorce more profitable than inertia.'

'I wonder about the name.'

'Of course, no one here would call a kid that name, only some foreigner,' and she sniffs.

I say, '*Lèse majesté*.'

'Lays trouble down.'

We ponder this, and then she says, 'About your prize. Just change the name, from "Piece" to "Peace", you needn't change the sound – and have it done before the Vatican, the Square! – there's always people there who sing, and you'll hide the sound of digging underneath.'

'No, no,' I say, 'that's quite the wrong effect. Besides, I don't want that monsignor around, although he's everywhere, a spider on the ceiling, bug beneath the floor – but no! those hands, that frock ...'

'Music is music anywhere,' she says, and then Romano's here, and full of something, bitter aphorisms, I've no doubt.

He says, 'Those priests, they've one thing right – emotion, passion's in the brain and heart. Reason, on the other hand, is calculation. And where's the seat of calculation? In your pants. Below the waist.' We hear him out.

*

'*Simplicissimus* – an oratorio in scenes and interludes, for reciter, high voice, and instrumental ensemble'.

'Then,' I say, 'a subtitle, "lamentations on three hunded years of war".'

I explain – 'The hero vagabonded through the Thirty Years' War, you may recall.'

'Four hundred years of war, then,' says Lola.

'Five hundred,' says Venus. 'You want it to last, don't you?'

'Who's is the high voice,' asks Lola.

'Right first time,' I say.

Venus says, 'Vagabond is tacky – make it mercenary. Conscript.'

Lola says, 'They had horses then. Make it Uneasy Rider.'

'This isn't a collective work,' I say. 'And Lola, if you didn't read this at school too, let me expound.'

'No, we didn't,' says Lola. 'We didn't even get to volume four of the Collateral Campaign. The teacher said he hadn't finished writing it. Then he got fired, for something else – like Romano said, too much calculation in his pants.'

'He can't have written it,' I say, 'unless you're much older than you look,' and she agrees:

'I found it rather fusty.'

'That's the trouble with eternal art,' Venus adds. 'And who's to be reciter?'

'Well,' I say, 'I thought, for the money, Venus – and the costumes too,' and she reacts.

'Schemer – all planned, you thought? You'd make a Venus trap!'

We turn away, she always spoils the party.

'Scene two,' I say, 'how Simplicius escapes a hit squad of Italians, and is adopted by some Turks. Scene three: is sold as slave, into a chrome-plating works. I saw a guy once, he worked there, went yellow, and then green. I never forgot – a lighting opportunity.'

'You've not escaped from anything so far,' Venus says.

'What's this scene one?' Lola asks.

'It's growing up,' I say.

'It seems it's all concerning you,' Venus says, 'and so the growing up scene's better left till last, an optional, maybe left out entirely. And what's this stuff with war? This sad old tune – there is no staler theme, and who is for it, war, until they get their boots and all march off and don't come back. Try another track, old vagabond.'

It's quite an irritation, but I feel she's right. I say, 'Well, there's the witches, fortunes won and lost, and luck and hermits, Jupiter as well, prisons and food, Croats – you bet – and no hard feeling. Slavery and peace and guns. We're all in it, like it or not.'

Venus says, 'That's not the point. It's dull. And screechy. Lola doesn't sing unless she's under running water – everything is backwards from the start.' She goes on, 'I'll be quite kind. You're wrong to start with it all written down – war and peace, wandering towards a resolution, all that – you need another kind of peace, not politics, but satisfaction with going on, eternal vagabondage.'

'No, no,' I say, 'it's true, desire satisfied is just a void. But your continuity, eternal voyaging, is just another kind of satisfaction. When I have a shape in mind, it's quite abstract. Nothing to do with boring immortality.'

She loses interest. I push on, 'Music seems to want to start with ends in its beginnings – the theme, the big idea, meandering to its end, the text belittled and belittling. All is determined – rivers know they end up in the sea,' but she's lost interest absolutely.

I think that Venus never ends, but must be worshipped by the guys who die, death is the pepper in the sauce.

*

'How's your village lad?' I ask. 'Seems well turned-out – hours before the mirror, sizing himself up.'

'I love narcissists,' Venus says, 'no mystery, they know themselves, so they don't spin off on you.'

I ask, 'Those parties your father gives – does your boy go? Do you have the guys all wearing masks?'

'Romano doesn't want people having a good time, he wants them being loyal, paid up. It's the being all together.'

'I don't want it,' I say. 'Don't feel the need.'

'So don't,' she says, 'and see who cares. Just pay your debts. If you don't obey, then pay – that's justice.'

I say, 'You know I can't, just now. Justice isn't part of it.'

I ask her, 'How's your father's projects?'

'There's trouble there,' she says. 'The bad guys think he wants a pantheon of deities quite new, but weak. They'd accept each others' gods and rank them as some minor prophets – but won't give up on their Big Chief. They don't believe that if there was Big God, belief is all the same, for everyone.

Otherwise – the movement of the warring peoples goes quite well. The guys who don't have water go and work in places where it rains, the waterful then take their ease and holidays, wherever there's no water, lots of sun.'

'How do they think to manage that, to carry on?' I ask.

It's disingenuous, and she says, 'They take the water with them – those little bottles that they carry everywhere, for sure you've seen them? And, at the last, the bad guys put some pressure on, and off they go in millions. Somewhere,' and she waves a hand.

'It all sounds neat,' I say. 'But this religion, culture stuff – it's true, the crazy things that people do and eat, are what can make it interesting, the world. The rest is making things and selling them, and getting rich or staying poor, or if you've nothing left to sell, well, there you are! It must be our biology that makes us do so well with Capital, but all the other stuff – the books and feasts,

and passing people under tombs to cure their devils, is –
well, it's interesting.'

'It's interesting but not true,' says Venus sharply, and
she hoists her drape. 'And you should think of finding
cash, your hermit's room is not enough! My father's
short of cash, and so ...'

And so, I think of playing bars, those twilight
afternoons in lounges, all those sets, the drinks and
insults, sometimes there's a fight, though hard to harm
pianos, though I guess you could ...

It's my America. I say, 'I'll need a stripper. And some
other guys. And electricity. And lights, a nice blue light,
so when she strips, she's like a marble, underground, a
mask with arms and legs, the guys get tranquil, blood is
frozen, and her moves are like a sleepy snake's, rising
before the altar where there's no desire, just afternoon
routine—'

'You'd best ask Lola,' Venus interrupts, 'she's the
one,' and Lola says she'll do it, only not direct, not on the
stage, we'll rig her up a feed, way in the back
somewhere, it'll be her, but on a screen, and so her
modesty is saved, she thinks, and it should be just that – a
ritual of modesty.

Venus says, 'I don't think they have that kind of bar
any more.'

'What do guys do in the afternoons, then?'

'They watch old football matches.'

*

Lola's disturbed – the threats, the debts, Romano's schemes, it seems it's new to her, how things here work, she asks, 'Should you tell someone about this?'

'Tell who? Why?'

'I don't want to end up with sadness, like Venus.'

'Most people are sad because the days go by, and she is sad because they don't. Anyway, she's over it. The mask business keeps her busy.'

'Bayan must have a kink. Those fires.'

'It's realism. They burn before they fall, structures, the space. Everyone's content – permission's easy for this temporary stuff.'

Lola says, 'I've nothing much – myself. A little to pass to you, I call it love, who knows, what it is to you.'

'That's pathetic,' I say, and we're silent.

Then she presses on, 'Venus now – that boy's not much, the family has land, they're well regarded.'

I think of fortunes and ask, 'What do they want with land?'

'To sell, of course. But she's not looking for a place to settle, just passing time, the masks and drapes, it's nothing permanent, nothing you can't slip off.'

I say, 'These ties and trusts, they don't hold now. It's transition – something will turn up, for sure. I'm sure,' and think of blue light, where nothing turns.

*

I must redress, I say, 'You're very sweet, Lola.'

'But sticky. That's it! You don't know what to do with me.'

I change the subject: 'We're not monogamous, as animals go.'

'What's that to do with it? Life can't be all couscous and burek.'

'Mine is. And human solidarity, of course.'

'I've not much else, aside from feelings.'

I want to say, 'Then hoard them up, charge interest, keep them for yourself and your old age,' but I don't. I say, 'Yes, it's not love that makes things go round – it's gravity, or sometimes alcohol and drugs, and coins that's usually round ...'

And in she jumps, 'But ingots are just lumps, heavy, hard to carry – as you've often said.'

It's true.

'It's not that I don't feel,' I say carefully, 'It's that the humanistic stuff kicks in only at the end, when it's too late, when people are at their last gasp. *In extremis*,' and I think of that old prof, where Venus first approached me – 'why is everything as it is' – lunch was the answer then, and if our circumstances had been reduced, and not had lectures to drop into, it would be 'food', not 'lunch' the answer – and we were fortunate at that time, before I had my debts, the ejector seat, all that, and so I float away from her.

'It's Venus,' Lola says. 'You desire her.'

'No, no,' I say, 'she's got that guy, the one with family and real estate – it's my desire I want. If we're not a monogamous band, then it's desire we have, dissatisfied, unsatisfied.'

Until the end. The end we've just concocted for ourselves.

Desire and jealousy, these are my drugs, my rock and roll, that place me in the human race.

*

The armies are manoeuvring. No one is put to the sword.

'Romano's not a father,' Venus says, 'not even a bad father.'

He invites me to a banquet: 'You could make a choir from my affiliates,' he says.

It's almost flattering, and Venus says, 'You may feel useful, but the money's always in his heart – unless you turn it into something else – loyalty, flattery, perhaps. Give him the philosopher's stone – not to make gold, but as an ornament, for his desk.'

'It disgusts me,' I say.

'Then live with it.'

*

Venus is at the banquet, and she says, 'It's not about clothes – the clothes don't come from me, but from the body. They expose. Like your songs, and so on – from the body.'

I'm quite bemused. 'Too much body, and our hunting fathers would get swallowed by the beasts.'

'So,' she says, 'give each person some cry, some signal, like each animal has,' and I reflect, two thousand voices is a jungle anyway, a crowd that roars on nothing, on no beach, no branch, no roots. Nothing. Maybe I've got it wrong. Wanting a shape, a structure – then these bodies come, attached.

'And wrong you are,' says Venus smugly. 'Look, there's Lola and my father – got together while you made distinctions,' and I know what the prof meant, that everything is as it is because I made it so.

We made it so.

Lola's at the banquet's head, sipping her gin just like a gipsy queen.

'Why did you do it?' I ask her, 'and with Romano – it's an incest, him being the father of my object of desire. Although you didn't give me time, just gave yourself!' and she cuts through this and says, 'It makes me the more interesting.'

I'm without words, and she goes on, 'When you've paid your debts, he'll set me up a Turkish restaurant.'

'It's a great idea,' I reply. 'I love great ideas. And meanwhile?'

'Meanwhile, I'm where you see – head of the table,' and with a scowl and pout and grin I see she's won approval from the company. Over and over going back you may work out the balances, all the finesse, that makes you loved – but here, it's just the usual grasping at the opportunity.

'You both deserve yourselves,' I say, 'but those debts! Romano's just a bank, and that's his business – debt.'

*

I've lost everything I never had.

Romano's a cork on the flood. He says, 'I could be anything – elected, manager, in business.'

'It's better what you are,' Venus says, 'a banker – you can fix anything. And then, there is your army.'

He laughs. 'Well, they've all got one, why not me? And here's my latest soldier.' He hugs me. 'I gave him Lola, now it's me the winner. A restaurant is always good for making cash, or losing it, and Lola's such a fleecy thing ...'

We all try to look happy with our lot, and Venus makes a sign – it's like she hones her powers, perhaps they're nothing special, but the game is this. When we were simple souls, we grew our greens and killed the lambs, and sometimes – Sacrifice! The price was modest, then came gasoline and radios, each one realised their inner selves, the root of being. No land, no power, but in our minds, each one an island, universe.

Venus and Romano, they've got power, and limits too – like the gods who strode around these parts, they hide behind the trees, the fountains. Those gods are dead, Romano goes on and on.

I say to Venus, 'You know how it ends – the humans just ran out of steam, of time. We've seen it end, we walk there.'

'No, it goes on. It's a shaded place, but there's still light, and visitors ...'

'You're wrong,' I say, 'you're wrong, you won't admit,' but she has moved away.

*

'It's odd about emotions,' I say. 'You can say – any feeling, love or hate, all that, up and down the scale, and no one can tell you "yes, it is," or "no, it isn't what you say you feel." We learn the words, but then, inside, from you to me to anyone, it's all a mystery.'

We're outside Lola's restaurant. I hesitate, and Venus says, 'Sure, they'll have burek, you cheap bastard.'

We see a bear – they say they dance, but they just lurch, as if each foot hurts worse than the other.

'They're not feet,' Venus says, 'we call them paws.'

I've seen them often, bears, on little boats, to and fro the Sweet Waters, maybe on their way to Kosovo. One bear may meet another, teamed up like guys and gals that used to haul the barges. That yellow fur, like old divans.

We hear a song from inside, 'Telephone, on the telephone' – like *Telgrafin tellerine*, it sounds like – it all goes back, the flocks of sheep for safety round the Blue Mosque, and Romano's here, he bustles up,

'It needs a touch, of class. I'll bring in some chunky girls,' he says.

Venus is on one arm, and Lola's on the other, it's a free and open scene. He says, 'It was Lola, bringing me that fruit, the Venus apple, cachi – brought a tear, the gesture ...'

So, that's where it ended up – she could have taken all three of them, the cachi, indescribable.

'It's all authentic,' Lola boasts, and I am glad for everyone.

*

Her restaurant – the menu says in tiny writing, 'Kurdish food at your own risk', it seems a cheap shot, but the place is filling up, affiliates and some who just seem tourists, and I'm deep in my *Simplicius*, and so we all look quite like vagabonds. I think of thirty years of war and wandering, then maybe we should think three hundred, even more as Venus says, that gives me lots of styles to play with – it's no more noble families, religion, territory – maybe war's over food and water, and I say quite loud, 'I do like Turks', and it is true, and some guy says, 'That isn't necessary.'

'I'm not Turkish, I'm Italian,' Lola says.

'I like us too,' I say – to play the fool – and there is laughter, and I go outside.

Romano tells me I've a little job. I buy a case, the kind they use to carry cash in movies, and he says, 'If you get caught, you don't exist,' and so it's airport, all that stuff.

Since I was burnt and purified in fire, there's no one who seems to think I'm dead. I say to Romano, 'No one believes a thing – when we reach the end, end of the world, in Rome we'll be the last to register, no one disappears here, disbelief will keep us going,' and he says to cut the crap, the word's obey and not believe.

*

The airport:

They strip us naked, put our shoes in heaps – and naked we can see how time works well – there's guys that look as if they've had their autopsies, and some with plastic shields all round to keep stuff in. The crowd is shuffling round, and there's a cheeping, quite subdued, it's us, a sound that's like a box of Easter chicks, and I think of that chicken, slaughtered on the road – the entrails thrown away and not consulted. There's guys that's all wired up that tick like longcase clocks – and Venus should be here with drapes or masks. I understand her job's to clothe the changing time – the past and future, they're intangible, the present, grasp it – whoops! it's gone – but decency requires you throw a sheet, a length of silk, to give some continuity, and cover up. We straggle round, for sure the bird of wisdom's not come out by day – they load us in the fuselage with stunted wings. We're all still naked, but I've found my shoes, or some that look alike, the pilot's in his clothes, a jokey guy.

He says, 'I can't remember if I filled her up with gasoline, I'd like you all to give a bit of cash so I can check and if ...' and we're all nude as eggs here, not a pocket, not a coin – and then we're tilted up – maybe that's a joke, about the gasoline – we're blasted off, and then swoop down, just like a set of eaglets – and we're here.

Inside a shoe, I have a little square of plastic, blank and empty, but there is a little hole. Romano told me I must memorise a chain of numbers, twenty-four.

'You're crazy', I said.

'If you forget,' he said, 'you don't exist.'

Here they have a concert, all is improvised, the local guys hoist in their instruments, like bits that's fallen off farm gates, and they sing songs in maybe different dialects, and some three hundred verses, and it's marvellous, but long.

What I have is two tone rows, I wrote the numbers down, and made them make a tune – twelve go that way, the other twelve's the first row inverted, coming back – it lasts perhaps twelve seconds, it's quite catchy and all day these guys, my colleagues, walk around the town, just humming it and when they see me, it is compliments that's maybe meant.

I think, next time you're in a concert and the twelve-toners come along, just try it in your bancomat, you never know, but here I guess there's some affiliates, they put my number and the plastic square in a machine like it's for selling drinks, they press for Sergeant Pepper, though the drink should surely be a Doctor P – they shoulder me away and money comes, and I have done my job.

When I'm home, Romano's pleased, and says my debt is less, and if that's crime, it's easy nowadays, the hard part being nude and searching for your shoes.

I feel the politics, just like the crime, eludes me. In the restaurant, there's always big guys being victims, and they tell you how their people's suffering, and you believe them, and then others, telling you that no! you don't understand a spit, the shoes is on the other one. And certainly, what's right is everywhere.

I say, 'No, one thing I know, the politics is quite beyond me, I don't read enough.'

'No,' the guys say, 'it isn't books you need but suffering.'

Romano is ramping up the public tree, he will be president, or butler to the palace, some such thing. He's had his life cleaned out, it takes some hours, a ceremony with guys in fur, some priests, even my monsignor comes flitting round. It seems to be a public man you have to live again, quite purified of all your tricks, they even do mock sacrifice, and then you're born again, and all forget. So, that way, you're immortal. A great relief all round.

*

We're all at Romano's purification – it's like a witches dance. They hold it in a bar, quite near the Vatican, but where the digging can't be heard. There's that monsignor, he says it's just a graveyard for the papal pets, a catty-tomb, a 'gatti-tomba', he says, and laughs – the first laugh I remember. Here's the pontifex, with reed and whip, he zaps the other devils with his weapon, and they howl, out come the names of many deities and demons, it's quite a multicultural display, though Venus seems a bit put out.

I tell her, 'Just our Christian civilisation coming through,' but miffed she is, and here come loons with bells, and want blood sacrifice – it's up to me, I have the biggest debts, the highest interest, they whisper that it's all a symbol, just flay yourself a bit, and no hard feelings.

'It's all symbolic,' I say, 'maybe you could do it to yourselves.'

Romano scowls and says, 'It's easy to be simple like you are – it's being *very* simple, or the highest simpleton, that's hard,' and I agree, there's no choice but to be simple, as it's all transparent, they're all in bubbles, glass all round, just like Venus and her sadness bubble, although hers has burst.

*

The monsignor reminds me – 'That concert, with the faithful,' and I tell him that I hope they're faithful to my music, not to clan or family.

'What's it to you?' he says. 'The serious stuff is seeing that we've air to breathe – the rest is witches' dance,' and I'm surprised they let him say as much, but then, of course, he knows where old priests go, they're underfoot and no one sheds a tear, their kids don't want to know them, in the grave there is no music – but I think, 'maybe I'll pipe some down, some koyré – cheer them up and open out another world ...' Now –

Romano's pure. No crime, no punishment. Elected he can be, and is. His past is nursery, the affiliates exchange a kiss, Turks and Italians, the gangs embrace, there's holding hands, and patting goes all over, whether it's for sex or guns.

'Another world is opened up,' Venus says.

I wonder if the mask of wisdom has been claimed and then I see – the priests and demons, scarlet, viridian, pigeon grey and crocus yellow – their drapes are her design. And so her world has opened up, and Lola's too, and burek looks like pizza, and our civilisation's one. We eat and kiss and hug.

Romano stands up on the bar and says, 'We're here to stay, the pure and less, we'll rampage through this city, bearing purity,' and there's a roar, and fists are raised and hands outstretched, and left and right are happy roaring, differences forgot – unity is good, it's what we strive for, I suppose, and off they go to seek out who they've business with, and debts.

*

In the village I see Bayan. In his basket, there's an egg, a mushroom, a pork kidney. An apple, other stuff, a celery.

'What's in that can?' I ask.

'It's what it says. Firelight. Quite characteristic and suggestive. These other things,' he says, lifting out an eggplant, 'My models.'

'How do you get clients,' I ask, 'when it's all ephemeral and at a loss?'

'The rich guys love a bad guy who's got class. And has a name and little things organic a committee recognises.'

'About the name,' I say. 'It can't mean much.'

'It does to Mongolians,' he says. 'Another desperate land!'

*

'You'll do your concert,' expansively Romano says, 'The monsignor will clear the space, put out the chairs.'

I'll have to write the music.

First, all round the square, atop the colonnade, we'll have the trumpeters. Then, I think, an African band, and some of Romano's chunky girls to give the movement, the choir – at least two thousand, heads all down and reading, so quite soft and puzzled. Batteries of drums, a gong two metres wide – the bells are there already, maybe Lola sings her song, 'the lost fiancée' – the lost grasshopper, dawn on the mountain, rising to kiss your soul.

I have the movements ready in my mind – the first, 'Credit Unlimited' – with numbers that will send affiliates to try them in the banks. But for the rest, with normal memories, a flux like stars, seeming random but fixed and nice, so's not to steal illumination from a neighbour.

Then *Simplicissimus*. Must he become a hermit, as it says? No real response to all the horrors, just some quick laughs and running off – but he's the lucky one, most idiots end up on the cart, with legs and arms just flopping there, so maybe I have more time – a little Light Show, of what's underneath the square, bodies of the useless and the infidel, and how the fashion turns! The dead will be in masks like Venus makes, then there's a section, *con eleganza* – birds of wisdom here, repeated, there are hundreds, maybe thousands, what a laugh, and monsignor could give a sign, a gesture, even benediction.

The last movement – naturally, I call it 'After the End'. We're here and back again, the voices roar and shriek – that's what it says, the score ends here, but they must not – the noise goes on, it all comes down, the sky goes indigo, the great dome shakes and splits, half egg without a chick inside. The figures on the facade, they twist and twirl, there's clockwork in their base, they've not enjoyed themselves so much for centuries – the earth is cracking open, up there rise – not reborn guys, for what did you expect? – but ghostly vaporised swirling things, like lengths of silk unwound.

Howl away! you thousand thousand amateurs! Romano on his throne (we'll rent him one) will lead the chant. So, all falls down, the great basilica is tumbled in the hole in front, the tourists are all careful and alarmed – they step away, and back a little – where the watersellers used to stand and sell those little hats to keep the cancer off – but now it's all gone down, no water, not much sun or rain, just twilight coming, never goes away.

The sound goes on, it must. The end has come, there is an after, time is running like the movie when you've gone outside. After the End. Magnificent.

Venus brings the bird of wisdom, real this time. It perches on her arm, and looks and sings. Remarkable. Magnificent.

*

'Magnificent' the papers say. Romano owns them, so it isn't worth a spit, but I am pleased, and secretly I cut the praises out and think to frame them.

Then – of course, I haven't done the show, it's all inside, and wonderful, magnificent, but like emotion – all inside. You must think, that as I say it, it is real, like love and being faithful. All the things you promised and solicited.

*

When I tell her, Lola says, 'Well, I like the bird part.'

I say, 'When the people all sing their different songs, it's dawn. A wonderful chorus.'

'I can't wait to hear it,' she says, politely.

Something wrong there, between us – but what's between us, is always space – and anything that's in that space between is usually other guys or gals. So – not much to be done.

'How does Romano do his bad stuff now?' I ask Lola.

'He watches while his people do it. Nothing's changed. He moves the populations round, he lets you in, he ships you out, he takes your cash, he gives it back. There's all of them that do it so, and say it's good – if not for you, then for another guy, a brother, even sister. What do you expect, it's always this. He adds the interest to your debt, but you pay in notes he prints.'

*

That monsignor is sliding up and down our lives. He always thinks religion, what a job, I guess it's better than selling spades.

He says, 'If there's no Big God, maybe there are lots of little ones, just like the ancient peoples said, and even tiny ones that fit into a jar or bottle, and they walk around and ask for reverence, screw up your life,' and he looks at Venus, and I think, 'the old misogynist, his disappointment's bad as his illusions were,' and he goes on and on, a-dancing on his dime.

Venus laughs, and says that we can worship her, but not too distantly, she likes the crack of folding knees, for once she seems quite human in her vanity.

XI

I'd like, I'd hope, to walk with Venus, in that flat land, when all the rest has fallen down and gone: gone all those tired and thirsty places, the people starved or suffocating, and where Romano's run his course, my debt's paid back, or else forgotten, never having been written down. Blue light.

She says, 'I've too much on. Go on your own. And if you want, the mask, the bird of wisdom mask – it's yours.'

I tell her, 'No, Venus. That would look absurd, there's no one there to see, no birds, no nothing. There was always you, alongside. The object of desire. No mask. For if I'm on my own, desire is always there, inside,' and then I think, it isn't much, but everything there is, and that is why it is.

*

The blue light's thick, like dust of ground-up quartz. There's no one left, some shops are shuttered up, against no thieves. Here, a blue river, a blue road. The grass is blue, like grass in moonlight, but there is no moon. Dark blue some bridges, and no sound. 'No blues,' I think, and laugh aloud, a laugh that spreads around, blue wedge in a blue round. There's peace, but nothing to be done. Shame that it ended so, with nothing for me here.

*

Romano says, 'Now, don't forget, your concert's due, reviews are written, chairs are set. The diggers underneath the Vatican are halted for a while.'

'When is it?' I ask. 'My concert.'

'Tomorrow,' he says.

'That's too soon.'

'Then soon,' he says. 'You'll do it soon.'

STARTING OVER

'La privation de la vision béatifique
est le degré zéro du Purgatoire.'

Jacques le Goff, *Le temps du Purgatoire*

'And Nadab and Abihu, the sons of Aaron, took either of them his censer, and put fire therein, and put incense thereon, and offered strange fire before the Lord, which he commanded them not.

And there went out fire from the Lord, and devoured them, and they died before the Lord.'

Leviticus 10, 1-2

'Why clothe them? When they wear clothes and are under the moral law, they will assume an immense pride, a vile hypocrisy, and an excessive cruelty.'

Anatole France, *Penguin Island*

There's the crucifix on the wall. I'm back.

The surgeon, Dr Slavoj, says, 'We'd time to kill, so we fitted you up.'

I say, 'I thought it was simple, a thing – below the neck.'

'We found lots of things you hadn't mentioned – scars, holes.'

'The brain, the brain!' I shout.

'That always needs a tidy.'

I look around the room for demons excised, discarded, wooden toys – there's nothing. He's exultant: 'We took lots out, and put lots in.'

'But I'm still me?'

'And who would that be? How would we know? How would you know?'

I guess the head always has you saying 'me', and answering too – even if it seems a stranger. Stranger right now it seems – the feet don't flap, the fingers droop, there's gauze to stop stuff falling out – and there's a cup with things – they're beetles! Leechlike things!

The Doctor says, 'Just body acting up. The brain's the thing. We're artisans, you know. Don't just fit in some bits we find, lying around. It's like making a pot.'

The nurse says, 'Like making a tea service.'

I ask, 'When I came in, the world was coming to an end. We even thought of waiting – seeing if it did. So –

did it?'

And they laugh, as if I'm a Venusian, off the ship, feeling my way, making a joke. I ask, 'And memories?'

He says, 'You'll find they happen all the time. The moment passes into memory, and sometimes reappears, just like a ghost. You'll remember us, I think. The thing is to forget, forget your memories, the ones that prey on you and stop your healthy sleep.'

The nurse says, 'We gave you a big collectivity horizon.'

'Not communism!' I say and the two exchange a glance.

'No, no,' she says, 'We're men of science, women too.'

Slavoj says, 'Nothing to do with politics. All the players – us – have to think the same – somewhat the same – or else it wouldn't work. At all. Without the common land, it wouldn't be worth doing. Thinking, living. Couldn't do it.'

The nurse – isn't she a nurse? – says, 'Of course we have to think and do the same, or else there'd be no reason, and no universe,' and they chuckle together.

*

I feel it swaying. No, I'm not quite right, not yet. It sways, but not with those long, determined paces the elephants make when trotting. More like a camel, scenting something? Not a horse, that's clear, no kind of cart – if I could just reach out, I'd feel the leaves, the branches, the fat fruit, bold but friendly lizard running, flicking over the knuckles. The Sun! Seems to come and go, but always there, the worshipful, the venerable, our companion, up there it frolics through the fronds.

Bearers, a palanquin, perhaps. If you can tolerate the short life, the injustice – and that's just if you're rich! And now I hear those two, I'm back again, I ask, 'How much of me could you take off, and it still be me?'

The Doctor looks at me, little black eyes, 'You're the most interesting person I've met,' he says.

The nurse says, 'However much we took away, what was there, or added, what was left – would still be you. There's no one else it could be, every morning you'd greet it as yourself, and every night.'

'And if I die – is that still me, or are there missing bits? Or memories? In some head, lingering? Bits of that universe?'

The Doctor cocks his head. He's like the dog on the disc. 'You must have asked,' he says, 'If that old guy, maybe your father, dies, would it be good? or bad? or natural? even a relief. Or just what happens, just this one time, to someone who filled spaces in your life. You can't imagine a space, without this person, always there in just the right slots ... What's you, what's memory – where do your "other people" fit?'

The nurse says, 'When you see on TV, they're always brainwashing these actors and spooking the actresses – you never see a woman writer with a credit. Did you know, women have to use a pseudonym, a man's name – what do you make of that?'

I say, 'But memories ...'

The Doctor says, 'Ah yes, "memories are made of this". But what, exactly? Think of what you remember, then think – imagine – what you don't.'

The nurse says, 'There's plenty to go round.'

I insist, 'So, objectively, I consent to my death, as I do to other people's, to be part of the flux, the me that was always central, now no longer so – and for a reason that's outside, beyond ...? Like human sacrifice?'

The Doctor interrupts, 'Why outside?'

'You mean, that judgements are already, always, part of me, my little province?'

He says, 'You make your judgements about people, situations, that don't exist, that never have, that you have never seen nor known. It's in your head. Your kind of guy – he's underneath their bombs: their kind of guy – (who's quite like you) – is under yours. What makes you judge that yours, your guys, your bombs, are more deserving? Why, you don't know the issues ... once more, is it natural, or is it bad?'

The nurse nods, and checks off something on a pad. I think, '"Most interesting person" – that's what's on the protocol, they say that to all the guys, but after that, the "me" seems less alone. It even feels for others. Yet – the deaths of all! Not inconceivable, but maybe end of world is also end of reasoning. It's all quite complex, living – it seems at times there's moral calculation, others not; or else some scale, or else a protocol ...'

'Then, there's history,' I say. 'All full of people, thoughts and curiosities, quite unlike me – yet as like, and different, as all the other people still alive that I don't know and can or can't imagine, who live far off, short lives for rich and poor, and getting shorter ...'

They stare, encouraging, as if I'm taking my first infant's steps.

I insist again, 'They said the world was going to end. Well, did it?' and the two just laugh, a horrible open genuine laugh, as if it's really funny, they're amused at the idea and not at me, so any answer would be – well, would not be funny in the least.

'Well, well,' the Doctor says, laughter out of his mouth like spaghetti tails: 'This time you've really surpassed yourself. I always said, the most interesting –

now the wittiest, of all the persons, that I've ...'

Then, his black pupils like two black voids, he says, 'You see that guy?' and he points to another white coat, half hiding, half leaning behind a pillar. 'We're all trying to get rid of him. Life is that, even if you don't know answers.'

He shows me a questionnaire and says, 'I'll tell you how to answer.'

I see: 'Experience of cutting: do you find it terrifying? Erotic? Just familiar?'

'We get lots of knife cases here,' he says.

I disengage, but he does not: 'We see the brain,' he says, falling again into his profession, 'as a cultural landscape.'

The nurse says, 'We gave you extra hunter-gatherer, it brings the ladies in.'

I say, 'I'm more maso than macho,' but they go on:

'The moon of enlightenment – now, that's always hard. We cut out myth and faith – when you were over there, in no man's land, did you get some spark?'

'Zero.'

'Here, instead,' the Doctor says, 'we have a lively time. Music,' and he shuffles a step: 'Song,' and out comes 'September Song', half bleat, half bray.

'Cut the singing,' I tell him.

'Don't drive your car,' he says, 'we put in lots of rule-breaking.'

'So all the judgement,' I say, 'values, where has all that gone? Into that pile, with memory?' and the nurse tilts up her clipboard, and I see a sketch, a scribble, could be ethnic lunch, polyp with eyes, and then a space for Fun Time, and I see she's written '"Maso not macho" made us laugh to split.'

The Doctor says, 'All you guys we get in here, you love yourselves so tight, and ask if it's all over – the world – but never if you caused it, even a bit. You weren't away too long – we just tweaked "perception".'

'So,' I say, 'I can do the things now that before I didn't dare, or thought were not for me, or even anyone?'

And here's the nurse, she says, 'The choice is always yours. Evaluation – that's always the same. The rules, though – not always clear or straight.'

'The rules don't come in sets of two or three,' the Doctor says, and then it comes to me, the fear.

'I'm still a hetero?' I say. 'I'd got kind of used to sparring with the ladies,' and they laugh.

'Why, sure,' almost in duet they cry. 'Straight down the middle, that is where we put you.'

'Of course, we mean the middle of the hetero track,' the Doctor says, and I suppose I'm glad, and even thankful, though I'm not quite sure if normal tracks bring happiness or just another mystery.

*

The Doctor's eager, and he says, 'I went biking. Trail bike, on the Andes.'

'That will have been strenuous.'

'I took seeds. I gave them to the locals.'

'Tell me, then.'

'Cannabis. I persuaded them to plant pot instead of coca.'

'That must have been tough.'

'The moral objective's firm. A lesser evil to replace a greater one.'

I say, 'I'm not convinced you got the balance right. They were happy chewing, now they're smoking. They'll still complain about the chain of being and its consequences. Anyway, why are you telling me this?'

'I thought you might like to come with me.'

*

No one visits me – that's good. If they were old attachments, maybe this fresh brain would put them off. If they were new friends, I'd know continuity had been broken, old me departed, new me unrecognisable. All the same, it leaves a mystery – maybe I didn't tell some people I was coming in. And who were 'they'? Friends

from school? Army? Monastery? The corporation? –
friends are very much the same, and so are relatives –
and as I muse, here comes a face unrecognised: she asks,
'Are you there?'

'Absolutely.'

She says, 'I was curious,' now she's two people,
there's a silent man behind who pulls her back. She says,
'I'm not seeking you. I came to visit someone else, but
they've departed.'

'Hospitals are like that. I'm sorry.'

'Why do you think this is a hospital? White coats?
And clipboards?'

'Feeling ill,' I say.

Why has she poked herself in?

'The sign,' she laughs. Everyone here is fine at
laughing. If laughter were a sign of happiness or fun ...
but here, it's just the side of something else. Sadness.

She shows me the sign: 'No elephant rides,' it says.

*

I hear her call the guy she's with – 'Jake' – an eager
hound where moral mystery's concerned.

'This place here,' he says. 'Is holistic, first they fix
your body, then they talk you over. And they cut you too,
but only if you pay,' and so he points to a motto, a board

written in black pen: 'life is chronic, irreversible – but you can learn to live with it.'

He goes on, 'They've got the right end of the stick, these laughing guys and gals.'

I want to say, 'Sticks don't have right or wrong ends, or, if you prefer, they're quite indifferent.'

But he's jumped ahead, and says, 'The middle of the stick now, that makes it a fine fighting tool,' and he makes some stick play, tells some history and stuff we don't want to hear – about wicker armour, diets, bronze bells and such.

Here, on the floor, there's a bill. The head – 'Holistic decisions: moral and surgery'. Below, 'Easy terms'.

I ask the Doctor, 'Who makes these decisions?'

'Obviously,' he says, 'we all do, otherwise there'd be no contest, no game.'

'When it's decided, what do we do?'

'We here,' and his troupe giggles expectantly, 'do more or less what we think.'

'My head,' I say. 'What did you take out?'

'That again, still? Duplicate memories – lots of guys have almost identical pasts, and these cling on, they won't lie down or go away – so what's their point? School, play, growing ...'

'There's no point, I guess – but then, I'm not deciding...'

'Memory – in general, not a good basis for anything. Experience, now – but, there we find it's different for everyone, and then – it's here! it's gone! and back to memory, to fancy wafting free.'

I see lots of holes in their holism. Is the me I've got inside still adequate for walking up and down? The street, it looks like Tokyo, the hair – the red, the blue – those whores in gingham dresses, look twelve or less, but – yes, it could just be Japan, I seem to look like other people, and I say, 'Then I'll be off. Morality can wait, I'll go down in the street and show myself.'

'I'd hoped you'd come and bike with me, and spread the word,' the Doctor says. 'Of course, with pot they'd still be poor, but happy – better that than rich and lazy, don't you think? running guns, abusing kids or taking us as hostage.' He's anxious and he says, 'Better the cannabis, it calms you down,' and off they go, and soon the smoke comes thick and green – wafts from underneath their door, it clogs the keyhole, the yellow-green is in our ears and in our shoes. We linger, tranquil, waiting to decide the next important thing.

*

That Mae – she has a playful face, but striving bears her down, a weight like marble on her head. Her Jake's a wizened thing, brown and tough, a stone without a prune.

Hmmm – I could run off with Mae ...

Jake asks me, 'Will you go with him, with us?

'Is Mae coming?' I ask, avoiding my 'no'.

'We'd bring justice. Though Mae stands for freedom, rather – but we're catching up on it, with all the books.'

Jake makes raw documentaries, and Mae – 'Mae tells me where to point the eye,' says Jake. 'She knows a story, I just see what's beautiful.'

Now Slavoj says, 'You'll come with me, surely?'

'You're embarrassing me,' I say.

Slavoj says, 'It's because you don't like me? Don't know me?'

I don't answer. He goes on, 'If you knew me better, you might like me less. Even hatred. But the right thing is to do the right thing, don't you agree?'

Jake takes me aside, he chews words like he's stupid, but he's maybe slow, he says, 'They always put some super in – you know, you think it's all Montaigne, the human bit subordinate to some good sense that comes from who knows where – the super sets you up, makes you a fighter. It all takes off. The axe against the door, to set the prisoners free and scrambling down the walls, they're all in white – barge-haulers, cut them free. A divine fire!' And he cocks his head for the crackle.

Later, Jake says, 'If you touch Mae, I'll kill you.'

We get to chatting, and he shows me his scraggy knuckles, polished like Granny's and yellow as meerschaum, well kippered.

'Look at this!' he says. 'And this!' – and both arms are wearing armour. Plates. 'The hands. Lethal. With one blow,' and I think of whoever it was killed flies, just so. A terrible gift.

'The arms,' he says, 'in the Galapagos.'

'Those turtles are implacable. I hear,' I say.

'We drop over – from the Andes,' says Jake. 'They only let just one or two a year – a decade. I got these plates there – climbing rocks, and down they came.'

'He pulled the island down', I think.

'It's Mae who puts the ethics in,' he goes on. 'I am pretty fearless, as you see. It's she that knows to swivel – puts the moral camber on the slopes.'

And here is Mae. She says, 'He loves to boast,' but from me there isn't much for her to fear.

'The world,' I ask. 'It didn't end?'

She says, 'Those who are here, who're left – we need a clean: a reaming out of everything, of all the icky stuff, an irrigation of the mind, you understand.'

'A document. A movie – one that doesn't move, but lifts you up,' I say.

'Exactly,' she says.

I ask, 'That Jake's a biker too?'

She says, 'Slavoj put it in his head. He wanted a friend. It's quite incongruous. Jake's an auteur.' She's proud, but giggles.

*

I'm exactly the same as I was.

I'm not, of course. There's the mulch of time, and maybe they switched some bits around.

Slavoj says, 'Bit more right hemisphere, and you'll appreciate my verse. Bit more left, you'll see through Heidegger,' he and Janet ride the circuits in the heads, they're into literature, general conversation, and all that.

I still like Jake the maniac, his flat photographer's eye. And Mae's so sweet, desirable – she's an obsessive's groupie, I fantasise her into uniform. I could risk death from Jake, and maybe get off with a beating.

Janet the nurse – 'I'm not a nurse, I'm everybody's boss' – says to me, 'You're quite ready for the street, again.'

But no! Going back is not the deal (the world has ended anyway, I'm sure) – and now infinity is pulling. Shall it be biking up the Andes? Or something more original?

*

'Up there,' says the Doctor, Slavoj, 'from peak to peak – you hear every radio station in the world. Or there is none. There is no air, then there is wind. There is sulphur, rising in plumes like the wings of monster angels, your eyes water – then you see the pyramids, down there on the plain – the sacrifice, the service. Continuity! That is being someone, that's community, the great chain. Chosen by men to meet the gods,' and his eyes are far away, two black basalt points, dreaming of surgery divine, the humans sacrificed.

'Gods,' Janet says. 'Meet them or please them. Either way, it's a bridge. A highway. Us to them. Where did that world go?' she sighs. 'It's swept away, you just delve through the sweepings.'

It's a thought, it brings a tear, and it's the truth. Do you have to believe the truth? Is that what belief is for? Jake is listening, pauses in silence for a little while.

Then, 'That guy,' he whispers to me, admiringly, 'is set to be the biggest pusher in the New World – a veritable Cortès, Columbus, Raleigh, Drake, Pizarro – but noble too! Bringing not measles, taking not the common spud – instead, salvation! Away with the coca and its masters, no more the Indians lingering by the road, their little pokes of blueberries for sale. New Kings of Cannabis, empires of the weed. The cosmic bhang!'

And here's Slavoj, he says, 'It does you good, too, that

weed. Away the smelters and the dams, on, on laughter, and the rictus grin – Mother of God, that river – so portentous – away the foul degrading work, away the mine – recline! Peace, love and garlands.'

And Mae says, 'Just like before. Our fathers told us how it was, when peace and music brushed aside the nuclear dust, and all had heroes and a flag' – it's hard to stay unmoved, though it's all new to me – but then, my world is ended, that is clear, and from the ruins of the old, we build anew. New memories, new truths, and Jake has cyclist's legs, he'll make the trip, and several too, and Mae will put the ethics, moral law, into Jake's movies.

'A curiosity,' I ask, 'do you ask the local guys to maybe sacrifice themselves to make a point, for you to take a shot that says it all?'

'We never ask,' Jake says, 'but some will volunteer.'

Mae completes the ritual, says, 'It is a gift we offer them. To say their piece, their all. A bridge. A highway. Jake's just the crazy guy – he takes the shot, it's me who puts the ethics in,' and her face is set and firm, she's righteous, you can tell, belief and truth are one for her.

I say, 'Some time I'd like to see your work.'

*

They needed this, my interest. It fires them up.

'Memory ok?' asks Jake.

'Worlds end every minute,' I say. 'Memory? A broken pot.'

'Don't yellow-dog me,' he snarls, 'feller, same for you is same for all.'

Mae hushes him. She says, 'Memory and judgement must be the same for all, or else our movies would appear quite different to everyone, and so the moral law would lose its point. Just an opinion, leading nowhere. We're not bigots, but to build – you must start from the foundations,' and down the street we lurch, we three, Jake leaping up to grab at signs until his hands – yes, even his – are bleeding. Mae and I entwined, we are the two firm legs of our wobbly stool, Jake's the long and short leg as his fancy drives. I see a beautiful girl. She licks an ice, her tongue is long and thin and red, and in her other hand, a spliff.

I think of Doctor Slavoj, say to her, 'Smoke gets in your history.'

'Fuck off,' she says. Her tongue sounds numb.

Mae says, 'That's good, she'll not report you, no molesting – you won't go to jail,' and I think – their camera gives immunity, for nearly everyone is keen to end on film, though cut and mute, and trusting Mae to give them resonance and words of goodness.

*

I ask Slavoj, 'Doctor, what goes into your remedy? That girl's tongue – like a serpent's.'

'My, what a genius you are!' he says. 'Synthetic pot, it doesn't coat your tongue, and not for hedonism, but to forget. That play, remember, where they put juice in everyone's eyes? Made them all forget. That was a trivial thing. My aim now ...' and he's ingratiating, 'Just think, you've nothing running through your head. You go about your day, like it's on TV. But others now, your neighbours – some are taken off by guys in uniform, they cut them up, the bits thrown to the pigs, the dogs. How can you live with this – you being normal, and beside you – atrocity! For you, for them, the magic juice. Forgetfulness. *Mann vergisst* – it is my magic gift – oblivion. To start again.'

I say, 'That's why I'm interesting? Because I don't remember ...'

'Maybe you don't,' he says. 'Maybe you do. At least you think the world has ended.'

'It's ending all the time,' I say abstractedly.

'Yes, but here you are,' he says.

And so, I guess, is Mae and Jake, and they are keen to try it all again.

*

Then, they're praying, down on their white knees, all clad in white, Slavoj and Janet:

'Oh Earth! who permits – the synthesis of weed, when all the rest has been mined out and penetrated. Oh Sun – betrayer – shine on our resurrection, shine on our Brother here, the interesting one –' and here they laugh, they must mean me, 'and Jake the fixer, Mae his moll, and bless the Starting Over, those who haven't grasped eternal reprise, the take-it-from-the-top, with all repeats! Bless us all, stuck in our grooves, seeking a mystery, not a truth. Passivity, not action but a drug that does no harm. Bless us all, and save us from the Great Helmsman, save us from the Great Gravedigger, save us from capital and from labour ...' and on they go.

So – perhaps it's true, it's all ended, here we are, or some of us – and Janet says, 'I love that prayer,' and Slavoj says, 'So long as it evokes real things and plans,' and they giggle together.

*

Here's Jake, in a huge receptacle, an intelligently designed waste bin, bullet-shaped, aluminum. It's a Wall of Death.

He's on his bike, triumphant. Slowly, and round and round, with a 'heeyar-hiyar', 'hi-yi-yicky-yicky', his bandana falls, Mae grips my arm, he's faster now, the thin legs whirr like electric fans, the wheels a fuzz of zero, and he's creeping up the wall, with swoops and drops, like a swallow in a chimney – 'Why's it called a wall of death?' I ask Mae and add 'It's a bowl of accident, at most.'

He's near the top, we hear the creak, the groan, the bike is at its limit, Jake is holding on – a parasite, a hard-cased flea, head is a hazelnut, seems the bike is dragging him up in teeters, down in a plunge – and wheeee, he's nearly up to touch.

Mae says, 'He risks, and so he tests the moral code. He risks his life, and asks for nothing. We should all try this – though maybe not the poor and sick. It gives autonomy – which if you haven't got, this biking will not give!'

'You're clear on that, at least.'

'Oh yes. That's Dr Janet's rule.'

I say, 'But Jake ignores the moral rule. Doctor Janet enforces it, but enforcement means you lose the choice. You cultivate your grass and take the consequences.'

'Yes, you put it in your pipe,' Mae adds.

And here comes Jake, his head is circling at the rim, he's horizontal and below there's a miasma, it's sweat of

Jake and farts, and trepidation, breakfast and lunch are in
there too, then …

*

There's a mixed conclusion, part plywood, clothes for
sure, and bike all mashed – leather, oil, the tires bite in
like drills – he's overtopped and some poor guy has taken
Jake and bike full in the thorax, and they're broken now,
all together, but Jake is fine and up, and now he's coming
round to all the watchers, waving a tin cup, miniatured
version of his wall, his bowl to beg with, 'Small change!
Big starts!'

Jake says, 'Don't mind the guy I pulped, I did the
work. I took the risk. Not through surgery, and my law is
not the moral law – I'm free! I'm unconstrained.'

'Except by laws of gravity,' Mae whispers.

Sharp as a cog, Jake's in, he says, 'Momentum,
darling – that's the word.'

*

Now they're off. The Andes. There goes Jake, the bike.
Slavoj and Janet, prostrating for a prayer, and bags of
seed and copper coils for brewing stuff, and Mae is here,
and she will stay.

So, Jake's outside the moral law, he follows accident and risk. And Mae applauds, but longs for order, and for power. Slavoj will make you good, but he will tweak you first, so you forget. Away with memories, they blur and blot. The moral law requires an open space to work upon, synthetic pot's the cure – consensus with a grin.

*

I think of Mae, and fantasise.

What's this? My head says 'Madame Bovary' – her skin, spotty as a fig pudding. And Mae too – refined tapioca underneath, and flecks of something sweet and pungent, and I think, 'Goddam – those doctors have me muddled up, instead of fantasies of sex, it all turns into food – and what is worse, it's food uneaten, unattainable. And here I am, I'm stuck on Mae, until some other dish is set before, a dessert in the desert, gorgonzola dreams – not that it's racism, for some crispy pork with cloves would do as well. It seems we've a taboo about blue food, so that excludes the Touaregs – though, thinking through, it isn't even plausible, for food taboos are what we most enjoy to violate.'

And so I muse.

The guy that Jake cut up, doing the circus act, now he's beside me, waves the Doctors off, and says, 'To sue would make me look ridiculous.'

I agree, and say, 'They're going far beyond our world, our law, to make another world, another law – so stand well back or else – the wall of death could well be yours. Jake took the risk, you took the fall, and that is life, rejoice, forget!'

*

'I like you,' says Mae, 'because you're quite short and not very bright.'

'My education,' I say to excuse myself.

'No, no,' she says. 'It's quite congenital – your parents can't have been bright, to have an unbright son like you.'

I think of sweetbreads with artichokes, and then of Jake, a-pedalling up and down her.

'Slavoj and Janet,' I say, 'they have some big task.'

'They're starting over,' Mae agrees. 'No more fantasy and brooding – they'll start a world in which you smoke, and you're relaxed, and then you do what you must do. What you are paid to do.'

I say, 'The peasants will all shoot, when they see they'll lose their land to grow the natural weed – and when Slavoj starts dumping his synthetic stuff, that needs tin sheds and hydro dams ...' but all the while I think of puddings hidden in the trees, of roasts by post, and love is all around, delightful kitchen smells.

'Only in wonderland,' Mae butts in, 'will you expect to find confected desserts in the forest – that's what Janet wants to stop. She sells the smoke that makes you dream – relax into the blank. Do what is correct,' and we both wonder where that leaves poor Jake, who lives his dreams.

'Jake!' Mae says, 'his bum's ground down like two quail eggs!' and we both laugh complicitly, to think of him there, above the clouds, ducking the stars and meteors, his little piston legs – titanium. The effort brings your brain to zero, and to rest.

*

'Plums,' says Mae. 'Not cannabis. That's so last century.'

'Why plums? And the serenity? The blankness?'

'Doctor Slavoj – he loves his tipple. The moral law, that's want they want. And booze, not cannabis. Wipe-out, not trance. No memory, and no experience, just do the good, tease out what is correct.'

'Jake's bike?'

'He takes it everywhere. Nothing to worry you.'

I say, 'The moral law – it seems like gravity for Jake.

If you don't pay it heed, it's just momentum takes you up. And if you live by day and day – then, you've no universe, not like us rich with little telephones and such. You'll love the speed, the swooping down, the roaring up – it takes you to the top, and even over. Free and damned.'

'And yet,' Mae smiles, 'it's what they want, those two, a moral law that works from day to day.'

'But accidents and custom do as well, or bad,' I say. 'And calculation too.'

She shrugs, and says, 'It all fell down. The lot, world, everything. So now – they feel it needs some ...'

She pauses, and I say, 'Reflection? Autopsy?'

'No – acceleration.' she says. 'Experiment, to see if it could happen differently.'

I'm silent, I accept, but Jake's bike bothers me. 'Jake?' I ask.

Mae says, 'He's the monkey. He scents blood, he seeks it out, we film it, and his racing tricks make cash – for us, for Janet and her crowd. I paste on the manners, as you know.'

'But he needs that cone-thing, the gravity.'

'There's always mountains, canyons – he goes everywhere. There's little upkeep.'

I want to ask, 'What's he like in bed?' but that is not appropriate. I ask, 'So, what's he like in bed?'

'He's cheap and cheerful, like our grannies used to say. All you could want. Besides, he is a hunter, not a gatherer – runs fast, and doesn't hoard.'

'Slavoj and Janet – to promulgate the moral law – must it be from mountain tops?'

'It's better so – it gives perspective – in the end, it's all to calm you down, submit, accept what you are given – the real bad ...' and she pauses, and I think she stops before she says 'bad monkeys' – thinking perhaps, humour and nostalgia for those scenes of figures scurrying, the horsemen cut them down – the greatest game, the hunt, the storm, all that – 'The moral law, to be obeyed, and not just fancy, needs its punishments, its cops and judges. Otherwise – who'd care?'

I say, 'Why booze, and not synthetic drugs?'

Mae says, 'Janet's the smoker, Slavoj's for the booze. It's personal taste. They did a deal. There's trouble there.'

I say, 'And yet they laugh, it spurts up out of them, like fountains on eternal cycles.'

She says, 'Of course it has to seem like fun, and give some satisfaction. Otherwise – who'd give a spit?'

*

Up the mountains they go, planting plum trees all the way, Slavoj and Janet, scattering the law, unburdened with those tombstones, stone tablets you can't swallow. Cycling the rings around them, their monkey humanoid, the film director, auteur Jake – his cosmological eyes that seek out corpses, dispossessions. Film it.

'It's such a lonely trip,' I say to Mae.

'They have each other,' she says. 'Though that's lonely too. Besides, the moral law – everyone knows what it is, it just has never stuck, attached itself. Maybe people now prefer some surgery.'

There she stands. I think of rice pudding, virginal, the skin untouched, to me a bit repulsive, but exciting nonetheless. Leek soup, or lobster flesh – more palatable than Bovary.

'Surgery takes the edge off,' I say. 'You switch those wires, and holy wars burst in, and purity of race or village, and off we go a-soldiering.'

'Well, you must do something with your life,' she says, 'not grow a shell,' and I think of those turtles, battling on their island.

*

A cassette arrives. Here's Janet, 'Hi Mae, and that guy you're with now. How's the weather there with you, and thank the Earth and Sun we still have weather! We survivors must give thanks – and now, I've record news. Jake scaled a peak –'

And here the tape leaps up, a jerky ride with lots of sky, multicoloured as it's now become, with dust and ash and atom stuff, sunsets all day, and Mae says, 'Hush! It's all imagination' and there's pause, and Jake has got to where he's going. Then – a wafting off. He's fallen, dropped – the world goes round and round, beneath, above, it's hard to say, and there's his head, the face a scream, the lips drawn thin like bacon rinds – then, swirling round and up and down – there's pyramids, and orchards now, and crops all desolate, and maize in stalks and drying on a shed. Janet's here again, and says, 'You see it all, a tragedy, no moral law could break his fall, he always lived by God and gravity and guess' – no difference made between all those, I think, and Janet says,

'Slavoj thinks the fall's inevitable, it happens all the time, but specially at birth and death, and in between you may survive, just as Jake did, as you must do when pedalling, crouched like a cricket, avoiding sin and crime as you must do when bicycling – the posture that is innocent and individual, but with no choice, no holy, no profane, and no commands, just head down, eyes on the horizon, round and round those legs,' and in the video we

see the world is wheeling round, and over it there's cycle
wheels that's circling like cogs from clocks that's telling
some short time, and then there's black and Jake is in the
hole.

Mae is shocked, and says, 'Jake made the wheels go
round. He's quite magnificent. His best reels yet, and not
a spot of blood and lymph, his last act cleansed of all that
yucky stuff.'

To comfort her, I say, 'That's a great act, great artist –
hard to beat that one,' although you get the same effect
by tossing down from buildings or a plane, a camera with
a little chute to steady it ... but I don't say, and surely
Mae knows how to get that same effect, and then there's
Janet's head, Slavoj's, – they're laughing as they say
goodbye, and 'to the next.' 'Regret, nostalgia, death –
nothing to do with us, who live by law, by moral law. It's
all a wall, quite blank, with no mean thing at all.'

Janet says, 'Jake never disappointed, never a foot went
wrong, though at the last misplaced a wheel; no victim,
no real fault. And after all, a start must have its end, and
every end its start.'

Mae, at once recovered, says, 'Of course, it's mostly
happenstance, this life. And risk – some court it, others
can't avoid. But on you plough, and all the others try the
same, each with the same approximations, mostly they
are apostates, until the thing gets tough and then you

maybe save yourself and screw the rest – but that's OK, you try again, it's like the song says, you try and try and try again ...' and I hum on, 'you're never tough enough.'

Mae says, 'It's rough, not tough. You see, it's not about you, it's about your behaviour in the bad stuff.'

*

'Poor Jake,' says Mae. 'Of course, this moral thing's a sell-out. Slavoj and his slivovitz, Janet too, sold to the goodness biz. Jake didn't fit, he wasn't what they wanted – though he made their cash. Instinct and risk – the deadliest, most effective things.'

'If they're a sell-out, Janet and Slavoj, then so are you!' I say, and she is cold, a-twisting in her dish, an invitation for the spoon, the fork.

'The moral stuff just says "be good",' she goes on, 'it is its own reward, and doing so, we all agree the code is this or maybe that, and so we do the good and life is smooth. And then comes one who disagrees, philosopher or king, and there go half the guys or more, they follow him, and down the whole thing goes. It's power. You have to whip the stragglers in ...'

'Mae, you look delicious,' I say, and I'm glad that Jake is absent, maybe not dead but getting there.

'It's power, it's power,' Mae repeats, 'and I want

some. Or lots,' and so adventure's on the table now, but power over who or what – and even why ...

I guess it's true, that power-hungry's not a phase but physiological, a need that guys whose circuits in the head are all skewed out must fill, and so I say, 'It's an adventure!'

She looks at me quite cold, and says, 'It's death, you fool.'

*

Mae says, 'We'll have to change this sex and food thing, if you're going to go to banquets. The embarrassment!'

She takes a prod from a pouch, says, 'The Egyptians did it, why shouldn't I?'

I say, 'Surely, I shouldn't feel it sharp?' She sticks the needle up my nose.

'We haven't time to think of booze to put you out again,' she says, 'to send you to your paradise.'

'It's just a garden, not a paradise,' I say, and think of dark Roumanian beer, but she is up my nose, and then I feel a twangling in the brains as she is joining this and cutting that, and those are bells! – I think 'Mascagni – operetta's quite the thing today, but vulgar,' and I say, 'I like vulgarity, small dose maybe.'

But Mae is busy with her tools and says, 'It's not

vulgarity if it doesn't come as second helpings,' and here come stars and birdsong, canyons, those tall blue naves with tall blue organs at the end that play like tidal waves that never come and fish so slippery that they're here and gone.

'I give up,' Mae says, 'it's all a mess.' She talks of ganglia and my nose is full of broken solder, so we write to Janet – here comes a postcard, on the front, the symbol, Jake's spinning wheels, the spokes a blur, the motto 'onward, not upward', and the pair of them, Janet, Slavoj, high on some mountain, lawgivers, a book, some pointing fingers, and a sign that gives admission charges – though there's nothing to admit, no confession makes a difference, and so I guess it's just you pay to see what you should do, what is correct – as if you didn't know – and down the track again you go, the cities of the plain await, and little booths there are, you take a shot of mescal and the world is bright and tolerant ... But there they are, the pair, solid as local gods, and twice as solemn.

The postcard says, 'Mae! Tweak him – we just got our sources mixed – or sauces, hahaha – a commonplace, a literary thing, this sex for food. Remote controls, that's all you need – you switch from porno to the cookery, the channels are abundant – and he is back again on track, right up the hetero middle, and with appetite,' she tries, it works, and I am back again in normal world, and Mae is beautiful, not for consumption, although she's white as mushrooms, or raw leeks – but just a simile, no more.

*

'Jake's trick,' says Mae, 'was being tricked. They set you up – they set him up – they say "to take this risk" and thanks will come, lives will be saved, and satisfaction general. But – you tumble down, and that's all part of it. A game, a metaphor, a paradox.'

'I know about metaphors,' I say, 'that's the trouble in my brain, that embalming needle up my nose – I know you want to help, but ...'

'It's that Slavoj,' she says. 'He tells you what to do, and what the consequences are. He doesn't say those consequences are not here, nor now, nor maybe ever, nor what you might recognise. It all gets muddled, people and times, taking the choice – is it the best, run to the library or the maquis, pen or gun?'

And I say, 'You're beautiful, you really are, when wrestling with these things.'

She's annoyed, and says, 'That's almost exactly what I don't want to hear.'

*

'They want to start a colony,' she says.

'An empire. Chivvying the peasants, stealing land, all that.'

'To make the right choices, you must take a risk,' Mae says.

'Jake took one,' I say.

'Jake didn't fit,' she says. 'Those fish-eye movies, showing only what he saw – that takes you nowhere, takes you back to instinct, habit, what they taught at school. Not that you cared then, and still less now.'

'I'm not engaged by plans and schemes like this,' I say. 'At least he didn't fall on anyone.'

'He left the symbol of the spinning wheels,' Mae agrees. 'The ancients said that justice was a goddess, and she left the earth, and went back home, up in the stars, and no one's ever heard from her. Astraea – like my sister, last we heard, she was in Seattle, but that's further than the stars,' and she looks glum.

Starting over. It doesn't seem like fun. Searching for Astraea, in the desert, on the moon or in a camp, a squat, a jail – or in the mountains, where they overlook the plain, where all feel free, and down below a white of feathers, wavelets – no, it's plum trees, their blossom whiteing everything, then the green, and purple fruit.

'You'd think there were volcanoes,' Mae says, 'but it's stills for slivovitz. No human sacrifice, no drugs –

except a little pot for Doctor Janet and her rites. Just healthy booze, large quantities, in those huge sheds – for socially cementing – forget the ego, socialise and drink.'

'It solves a lot of problems so,' I say, but Mae is not content.

'I'll tweak you more,' she says, 'and see if we can't do it better,' though I guess I'd settle for no needle up my nose, and since it ended once – the world – just let's forget the future and the perfect, leave it lie, let's not go back and trundle on, towards another future and another end, but Mae gets angry.

'No, no, you coward, onward,' she says, 'that's the trip we have to take,' and maybe Astraea's hiding somewhere, coward she. But then again, there's sex and appetite and history to satisfy, and we must eat and screw and leave inscriptions too, to show that we have been and gone.

*

'Empires start as colonies, deposits of wanderers, marauders,' says Mae, wisely. 'My – our – colony shan't be like theirs,' she waves a hand. 'Their Empire of the Sun. Which there isn't, or hardly, any more.'

'What's special about yours – ours?' I ask.

'Risk. Slavoj wants an area where the drink will take

you – like on a spacewalk – out beyond decisions, choices. A clock-out place, where alibis are never challenged, where the guards stand down. Peace – not perfect peace, for you awake – but paradise without the headaches and the diarrhoea. Time off, time out, no sin, and no remorse. It's your reward for doing right and being good. In my time, ours, instead – there's Risk. For ever on the edge, and always chancing. In memory of Jake.'

I think: 'Fuck Jake,' but do not say. There went another wanderer, spinning his wheels, his tales, his threats, his webs, like killer discs that cut you in the back.

Mae says, 'It's not just about being good. That's in all the books. Their empire, Slavoj's, Janet's, will all go sour, they'll lose the thread. The being good, the being drunk – the guys get bored, and then there's temperance, and guns, and blighted trees – and off we go!'

'How about communism?' I ask. 'It all starts there, and then goes wrong.'

'Yes, starts there, sort of, and ends quite somewhere else, sort of, out of control, the guys get screwed, there's history and hate, and then they've all got cars and guns – and here we are.'

I think, 'Perhaps it's Janet and Slavoj I prefer – the slow and shabby ride, forgetfulness – before the paint falls off, the gods are in the spaceships waiting for the launch. Mae's got these lost guys, messiahs maybe, or just found and lost, the system's open-ended too, but struggles on – Risk! Freedom! – here too the paint falls off, the tires go flat …'

'Remember,' says Mae. 'Sex. You can have it "needle up the nose", or else – I'll show you a good time, and you can feel you're loved, protected, if you must, in the good historic way, just like you see in caves and books,' and wow! she's sure desirable, although there's power to be worked out, labour divided too – but all the same, it's better than she tweaks your brain – though what it means, this sex, I cannot tell, it's more and less than slivovitz, I guess it's risk, but while it lasts, it's better than catastrophe and falling off your bike ...

And while I muse, she tells me of a fish that tastes of all fish, since the sea's too hot to breed in, and I think of the old invention, the bird with paws that's like a thousand birds, and ask, 'Did you invent it, or just contract it out?' and she says 'Silence' and I must go and spy on Janet and Slavoj, and all their enterprise.

*

Slavoj is sitting quite upright, in a blue leather armchair. There's a sign, 'Bodies we fix, brains are all the same,' but I see no instruments, no white coats.

By his elbow, there's a pitcher of plum brandy, and the smell of plums and distilling them is all around, on mountain top. There is a wooden board, it says, 'The Doctor is sober', on the other side, 'The Doctor is drunk'.

He's sober, and he points at me, and says, 'Ah – here he is again – the most interesting. The most normal. Would sell himself for sex. Not even count the minutes. Would sell the law for cuddles. And some flattery.'

*

'How'd you get up here?' Slavoj asks, without interest.

'Some guys carried me up.'

'That was risky. They might have dropped you. We don't use money.'

I say, 'I paid them.'

He looks more interested, 'With?'

'Gold and diamonds. I've got lots.'

'If this is an interview, you must pay me.'

Then Janet comes in, sits in the other blue chair. There is smoke about her, and her face is lightly cooked.

I ask, 'When you're both quite boiled, who takes the decisions?'

Slavoj is bored, he says, 'Why, that's where states come in. They substitute – the drunken king, the addled queen – it's in the books, you know.'

'What does everyone do here?' I ask.

'They gather plums,' Janet says. 'And process them. Sometimes – under the knife they go.'

I insist, 'What do you eat?'

She says, 'Oh this and that. And sandwiches. A lot.'

I say, 'Of course, the moral law is equal, just and universal, so you don't need lots of other stuff.'

'You know how people are,' she says, 'you give them jam, they look for jam to put on jam, and then some more.'

I say, 'Soldiers? Priests?'

Slavoj finishes off his jug, rouses himself, and says, 'We have all those, but under wraps. They're parasites, jam on our jam.'

Janet nods and nods and says, 'We're not like Mae – she's fidgety.'

'Just interest,' I ask, 'how shall I get down?'

Janet waves a hand: 'The bucket – it would not take you up, we've rules against the apostates, what Slavoj calls the "interesting ones".'

I protest: 'I've always followed moral law, unless it didn't suit or didn't work, or was too intricate,' and I think, 'Well, I never dropped Jake off the edge,' and then there's whirring and a click of oily wheels, Jake's wheels are framed like clocks, they're everywhere, and though they don't tell any time, they all go off together now and then.

The sun sets like a pot of goldfish leaping from a sea of orange paint.

'Stay, if you like,' the Doctors say. 'We'll have another party – victimless, of course, and no remorse. The headache's down to altitude, not booze, so don't blame us: nostalgia, if you feel it – that is up to you.'

They let me down in the bucket, the apostates' bucket. The wall is sheer, it has been a climbing wall. Small ceramic heads, some bearded, some with a ring in their nose, iron tails dangling – the rock face is miles high, to climb it must have taken days. The bucket hits the side and makes a sound that booms, bell-like, over the great expanse of – air. And far below, the orchards and the bees.

All kinds of lizard – orange ones, some striped in black and green, the little crusty geckos, blobs of mustard, pesto, left on plates and dried; umber drifts on palettes – stretched out and passive, waiting for the sun that they're designed for.

I think of what Slavoj had said – 'The Andes are manmade. We know, we think, so little of what they did, those former, those ancient men and women.'

'They must have had material and piled it up,' I said.

'Of course, not wholly manmade,' Slavoj said, a little slurred and dreamy, ready to comply. 'That would be nonsense, wouldn't it?' and laughed.

Janet, laughing too, mussed his hair and hugged him to her, and she smiled at me, and turned away, pretending that the smell, the booze, was strange and quite distasteful

'They have a kind of net,' she said, 'a network, that will catch them as they fall, or stop them falling wholly through, for when they're on the wall, but tied with belts, or ropes.'

She went on, 'We love Mae, naturally. She'd never do us wrong, and never has. But there's so few around, the people, once abundant, – now it's hard to find them, and they're puzzled, and a little slow, demoralised, you'll see, and so if Mae starts up another colony – we need to share them round. The hands. The subjects.'

'And after all,' I said, 'there's just one side, and we're all on it,' and she laughed, and shook her head, agree or disagree.

*

'Our friends?' asks Mae.

I'm back. It takes a while. Months, years. Less. I tell her, 'A monoculture. Short of labour.'

'We can import that brandy stuff and put it in our lamps.'

'A dumb idea,' I say.

'It's called doing a good turn. The moral law is one, you just work out the details. The light it throws – it's so romantic.'

'Don't do it,' I say.

'You're so hard on what I want. Besides, winching that bucket up and down! You need a tiny motor ...'

I say, 'Don't play those games. Wheedle with tears, and in the end we'll all be crying.' Leave the blossoms, don't put them in your hair – with the fruit you make a pie.

*

Down in the street, there's pools of guys. The ones that won't obey the law, or pick the fruit, and those who made a pass at Janet – if not good guys all, quite sympathetic, as they say. Kicked out, away, from Slavoj's colony.

'We'll have to shut them up. Imprison them,' says Mae.

'You can't.'

'Who says? The moral law ... besides, they're just a tribe, fit for a reservation somewhere,' and I see a vulgar history is ready with its claws, its chain of being, reproduction.

'If it satisfies you,' I say, 'I'll put a lock on the front

door,' and so we argue on, and I am right, but often banished, and my portrait, my head, is on and off the medals that she gives for conduct, – conduct that's not good, but just in line.

The problem of the guys outside remains. I say, 'They're free spirits. Risks they've maybe taken, but that's Jake's thing, risk – the great trick cyclist,' and I know I shouldn't mention Jake, who landed in a tree, perhaps, and waits to make a triumph, comeback, all bones mended, ready for another risk, another drop ...

'Don't wheedle in with freedom,' Mae shouts back. 'Risk isn't freedom, it's just calculated, that is why they say a thing's a calculated risk. It's happenstance.'

'Rubbish,' I say, but that doesn't help, she wants free spirits in a camp and to see what freedom does for them, and then we fall to laughing at the spirits – there they are, the Sliv from Slavoj, cases of it, and there's ads, 'you burn your candle at both ends? Slavoj's Sliv will give a lovelier light', and Mae is charmed.

I say, 'You're wrong,' and she says that's misogyny, perhaps she's right, but so am I – still right! – and so we laugh and fight, my brain is back to middle tracks, you have to have it set to rights when everything has fallen down, – and nothing much to do, but put more locks on the front door.

*

'You'll have to sort him out, that Slavoj,' says Mae. 'Those guys he sends us, criminals – and what of Jake, poor guy, a martyr to the heights,' and I object.

'Slavoj's still the king. And I'm not climbing up the wall – miles high, it's storming heaven.'

'Use the bucket, then. Pay someone.'

'No.'

'We're the risky ones, so we go far. We owe it to the principle, to everyone.'

I say, 'It's not the risk, it's the certainty. Not just falling – the wall is made for that. It's the vendetta.'

I picture him, Slavoj, slightly fuddled, in his sky-blue armchair, above the clouds, the steam that swirls above the stills. The fumes. Queen Janet. It's a scene full of charm and pathos, and I say, 'He's a good enough man.'

Mae's exasperated: 'He holds us back.'

*

I pay them, to take me up.

'You've got a nice deal here,' I tell Slavoj.

'Just bits of everything. The more bits you have, the more you miss having some whole thing.'

'There's surgery,' I say, though I don't believe.

'They all die in the end. And don't do much in the extra time. My hands do dances.'

'You shouldn't send us all those guys.'

'You do with them as you think fit. And as for Jake – maybe he got tired of skill, and thought, 'I'll try a fall.' There's nothing wrong in failing, falling – specially if you're tired of not.'

He's bored. And if he flies – off the rock, punishment for nothing, no crime, no resolution, just lives blundered and his own screwed up – so much can happen as you fall. Epiphany. The spirals bear you up, the lizards, curious – those double lids should make you pause – ceramics too: once a fine industry, exquisite imaginations, visible only as you fall, and can't record. Or in the bucket as it sounds the midday bell – winched upwards, the day's executioner, rising with his knife. The lucky guest with brandy in his paunch, descending.

Slavoj says, 'I didn't want to start it up – again. Just to be fairly good – and here I go,' and he leaps up, knocks his pitcher to the floor, and shouts and spits and screams – 'And here I am, with all the killing.'

To comfort him, I say, 'There's worse things. It should all balance, balance out. Anyone who's had a thought, or done a deed, will have some dead ones to their credit. That is how it goes. And that is how the judgement's made.'

*

'Things are getting worse, they're working out,' I say: 'There's nothing in the law that says you've got to talk things over,' and Slavoj starts to shake.

I say, 'But you really ought to come, and talk to Mae,' and Janet says he ought, his hair gets mussed again, and here we are, we clamber in the bucket.

Down we start to go. It's slow, it's very slow.

'Did you give the guy a tip?' asks Slavoj.

'No,' I say. 'I thought the honour of you being here, if not the precepts of the law itself ...'

Slavoj says, 'That's good for me, but not for you or us together,' and the winch creaks, the sky is far above, the ground too's far below, and bothers us the more.

He peers out, the lizards cluster, tongues suck the rope, and Slavoj screams, 'That one's a dragon!'

'No, no, it wears a ruff, but there's just smoke, there is no fire,' and we go slow and slow.

I shout, 'Hey, you up there,' and there comes back, 'Hey, you down there.'

Slavoj says, 'We warn them against deference and hierarchy. That's why they act a bit like scum. Besides, it's time for him to come off shift.'

I'm surprised and say, 'There are no clocks, so how ...?' and then those bike wheels start to whirr, and once again I think, 'Fuck Jake', for with the whirr we are supposed to pause and think of risk-free worlds, and I'm embarrassed, an apostate. Then a bottle flashes down, and Slavoj grabs at it – in vain.

We hear a woman's voice, she's arguing with the winchman, and she says, 'If you cut the rope, they'll die, and there's an end on it,' and here's a slow reply:

'But doing so may save other lives, for certainly there'll be others lost – we can't just have a law, we must decide, and do the likely thing,' and on they go.

The lizards cluster round, and Slavoj's shaking's worse, another bottle sparkles by.

We're desperate, I say, 'We need to sing! That's always been the way,' and for a while we think of what would be appropriate, and I see clear, and say, '*Moses und Aron*,' and off we go, he's Moses, naturally, and down the bucket goes, faster and faster, and it tips and shakes.

Slavoj says, 'There's nothing in the law that says you must discuss, or that the hardest cases yield to chat, in any case, it's the survivor who is right, the others are just casualties of language,' and of course he's right, survival and power together make a case. He makes his sort of threat. For him to talk with Mae's no use – and down we go, there's cursing up above, it seems the rope is stronger, faster, than her arms can hold.

He falls, of course he falls. The law condemns him, if he falls and kills some passer-by – especially if he saves himself, – but that is quite unlikely, we're far above the clouds, the brandy smell is sweet, and down he goes, a little spider – all his legs a-wriggling as he drops, and 'yeeeeooow' comes back like ectoplasm as he falls. He hits the clouds, they rock as he goes through, they're like plum blossom and they part, and far below I see the petals white, but I don't see him hit, or if he lands on someone sleeping underneath the tree. From far above, I hear the lady winching say, 'Oh shit', the bucket stops, I sway, some lizards come in with me, and I think how Mae will be relieved, not facing Slavoj. Then there'll be two angry queens, bereavement, all that stuff, and tantrums in the bedroom if I manage to get ...

'Get me down!' I shout, and whoosh, I'm down, and there's Slavoj, the envelope that's left of him – chaplets of glass around his head. All the bottles land down here. He's been embalmed already, not a drop of blood comes out, there's just a drip of juice distilled and now distilled a second time.

I find a little flask – quite Roman – fill it with his effluent, it's pure as tears, but better – you can drink it if you wish, in memory.

So, off I go, as no one saw if it was suicide or accident, or even giving him the push that solves his

paradox – if paradox there was, here is the law, here is
forgetfulness and freedom – but after all, as Moses all he
had to do was cart the stonework home. And this, Slavoj
had failed to do, being instead the modern way to
compromise and talk with Mae, and promise things he
didn't mean, not taking things just by the book, and build
a camp for all those rejects, maybe run it in a joint
administration.

'Slavoj has fallen,' I tell Mae, 'calling for you. And
Janet,' for these lies don't seem forbidden by the moral
law, they being for the best, for Mae and me.

I say, 'I took some risk, but in the end, poor Slavoj –
just signed off.'

Mae is angry. 'Now we've to deal with Janet, the
spoiled Calvinist, befogged in her mountaintop – just a
tricky bucket for communication ...' On she rants.

'Mae,' I say, 'you've got political skills and nothing
more. Those two had an activity – nothing splendid, that
is true. But we have nothing. We're just predators. If this
is "starting up again" – or as I prefer, it's "starting over"
– you'll have us all in uniform, and climbing walls, and
you the warrior queen,' and she is even angrier, I cast her
back to tapioca pudding mode. But that soft and passive
skin's dissolved! Now she's more thunderbird, and flaps
her wings, and flexes talons on the windowsill.

'Away, away,' she shouts, 'or I'll come down and

scatter you and eat your young,' and she is screaming at the rejects in the street, they're sunk in slivovitz and slink away, but they have written on our walls and door, and found us wanting – 'even the risky ones weigh in the balance', and there's not much sense, except that it's a threat, or prophecy.

'We have to do things right,' I say.

She's still angry and says, 'No end of fuss! Slavoj deceases when he's on your mission – I hear you're Aaron to his Moses, a role that irritates. I want no voice of god or gods a-piping round my doors, our banner's reason, firmly on the plain, leave Janet to the high and mighty mount ...'

I interrupt and say, 'Butchery and bonfires, not for me, that's what the priests do, and gathering in and clothes' design – the "bells of gold between the pomegranates – of blue, of purple, and of scarlet, and twined linen" – no, Mae, let's not take that route. Let temperance be our thing ...'

But she ignores good sense, and says, 'What can happen with those guys, down there on the street, no law and no abode, no faith, no offerings, just desert swarf? We'll have to make a tribe, the "tribe of a thousand tribes", pay them in booze, but rationed – that's your task!'

I'm not impressed. I say, 'You can't.'

'Why not?'

'It's not your business, certainly not mine. My brain got fixed, and I've no mind to make some history for you,' I turn away, but she is everywhere.

'You are my captain now. Courageous or not, you're all I've got. I'll call you Captain Cat, from climbing walls, and covering up your mess,' and now I see her monstrous wings unsheathed, the eagle eye – a power no captain cat, nor general cat, nor major even, could think to take home, pulsing in his jaws. I should have trusted to the bucket and the winch, to take us down together, Slavoj and I, and through the orchards stroll, our arm in arm, and talk of good lives and their ethic, questions of state. All that. And safe.

*

Then Mae beams and says – 'It's all beginning.'

'No, no,' I say. 'It's all ending. Let it end. We're tidying up. It's all been finished,' but Mae is going on.

'Janet up there, she can't have kids, the mountains are all built.'

I object, and say, 'She's got field hands, and they'll soon put together some kind of clock, a calendar, gold and diamonds – I gave them plenty – and they've got Jake, Slavoj in death. Jake haunts the fields, Slavoj, the drunken one, is deity of chance and wealth – Janet too, she's in the smoke, and says some funny things, goes on for hours, repeating stuff – she's blown her sets, the left and right, synapses ...' Then I pause, for I see Mae bubbling up, then I say, 'No, Mae, not that one, not the starting up, and burial mounds and horsemen, tanks and all that. I'm not an idiot, we shall serve our time, avoid the plagues, and in good time we'll die and be forgotten. Forgotten certainly, as all the rest will go, and there's an end, another end, to all.'

*

'Slavoj – he was the soul of wit,' sobs Janet.

I never heard him joke, but say, 'He could unleash a zinger. Yes,' and wait.

I want to make my peace with Janet, though I won't go up the wall as Mae had wanted.

We talk as we might have, many years ago – with two cans linked by infinite lengths of twine – she at the summit, I, down here, beneath a tree, some sounds that may be they're piped in, of fountains, peacocks white, invisible among the blossom. Blossom lasts for months or years, when there's no clocks, no urgency to pick the fruit.

I say, 'Slavoj was cut, so rightly from the cutting edge

he fell,' and laugh.

She ignores my joke, and says, 'He was the life, the hope.'

I remember him, sunk in his baggy chair, a prisoner, the moral laws severe – or else demanding arguments of such refinement, ending in such paradox, of 'hohum', or 'whoa – but then' – his brandy, his kaleidoscope, the purple fruit like murex, like jewels, like glass in appliqué ... I lose my thread.

*

Janet's twang comes down the string: 'You killed him. Bastard.'

I say, 'He fell. Like Jake.'

'Jake didn't fall,' she says. 'Was killed. Bastard,' and she must mean it was Slavoj. The doors of paradise flip open, shut. Like synapses. It comes back, the meddling with my head.

'Talking of life,' I say, 'how does it go up there?'

It seems to me there isn't much, but then she says, 'It's the not knowing, if we're past or future, where the present's taking us.'

Poor Janet.

*

I'm back. Again. With Mae.

She looks quite pregnant. That's a trick I hadn't mean to play – a future never calculated – but she's in triumph, Janet worsted, just some awkwardness to smooth away.

She says, 'The rejects – I can't stand them.'

'I am your captain,' I say. 'I shall do whatever comes into your mind.'

But it's not true, and she goes on, 'You tell a lot of lies, but I'm not sure about your motives, right and wrong, maybe, just being puzzled.'

Out comes the embalming needle, and she's waving it around.

I shut my nose and squawk, 'No tweaks! The brain must be inviolable, otherwise the moral law is just burnt hay.'

'No!' she shouts. 'You're wrong, it's all negotiable, tweaking is good until we've reached agreement on correctness.'

'You made poor Jake a monkey on his bike,' I say, as best I can, 'unless he's found some way, some form, of being back – you gave him death wish, and you had your way.'

She's appalled. 'It's all for you, you fool, your captaincy inevitable – the best, the most refined, must win out in the end. Slavoj knew! The plan was his – Jake fell. The plan was mine – you rose! Slavoj, the executioner – natural justice. Then – over he goes!' Her voice drops, she sheathes the needle, whispers, 'The project in its polished form – is mine.'

I back away, and think – from sea and mountain always comes some feisty people with their myths in place, children of heroes vanished, sea-spume in their hair, or shirts of feldspar. For a while they sort the problem out, deal with the rejects, lots of sacrifice. Maybe Mae herself will be revered, or sacrificed, or put in jail. Her child, or dodgy twins, her Remus, Cain ... her throne, her state ...

'That brain of yours,' she says, 'it's on the loose, it's just a gull that floats before the storm, that trims its wings to stay above the waves.'

She's right of course. I say, 'So, what's to do?'

'It's the start of a dynasty,' she says, and coyly, 'Captain Cat,' and musses my hair. Words fail, but actions become clear and urgent.

*

I fill Mae's car with slivovitz, and it soon fastens on the taste.

I search its little cupboards – a tiny pistol – here's a book of precepts. Let's see what it thinks of Mae's regime. It seems that I could run, or stay – diluting the catastrophes, it says – or try assassination.

Or just wait and see, consult wise men, and women too.

I drive slowly down the road, its red-packed earth is springy, and I stare around, it's like the elephant ride I'm not supposed to have. That's doctors' orders.

Jake's avenged with Slavoj's tumble, accidental murder, suicide – one score for justice, though I think I hear the rolling of the cosmic dice, and say aloud, 'Poor everyone.'

There's no one here. The manmade mountains, canals and canyons cut, some paths sliced through the rock, deep down. Fine heads of onions, gone to seed – it's all magnificent. No pomegranates for priests' aprons, all that to come, or else it's gone, just Janet, high above the clouds, no prophet she, and so destined for divinity.

She left a pack of seeds for me, she wrote, 'plant these, for memory'. It's pot. I throw the sealed pack from the car, we gather speed, the blue and purple, scarlet, weeds flash by – and now there's white and yellow, saffron, low bushes in the sand. Faster and faster, Mae is far behind, maybe there's someone like her coming nearer, out of sight for now ...

We're at the edge. I stand beside the car.

Below, so far beyond, the track twists down and turns and disappears – and there it is again, it takes its course anew, twists, turns, and disappears again.

There should be eagles here, maybe some rabbits, but the precept says – 'be patient'.

I give the car a push. It makes no fuss – I'm quite attached to it, it's dumb and true. Then, slowly down the path it goes, and follows round the curves, but doesn't make the twist, and disappears. It doesn't make a sound, and all is as it was before, it seems.

I can't stay here.

I turn and walk away, and walk, and walk.

About the author

John Fraser has lived in Rome since 1980. Previously, he worked in England and Canada.

www.ingramcontent.com/pod-product-compliance
Lightning Source LLC
Chambersburg PA
CBHW030305180626
46810CB00003B/928